PRAISE FOR *ALL MY NOBLE D̶———̶ ̶T̶H̶E̶N̶ WHAT HAPPENS*

★"As in the previous book, ̶————————̶ s, fashions, and conflicts of the era ̶————————̶ rs who represent multiple politic̶———————————̶ at insight into a nation vibrating with changing attitudes." — *Publishers Weekly*, starred review

PRAISE FOR *SMALL ACTS OF AMAZING COURAGE*

★"Whelan's insight into history and her characters' minds make every moment of this saga believable. The open-ended finale will leave fans yearning for a second installment."

—*Publishers Weekly*, starred review

"Set during a pivotal moment in Indian history, Whelan's vivid, episodic story explores the tension between doing what's right, rather than what's expected, and the infinite complexities of colonialism."

—*Booklist*

"This is a beautifully written, fascinating, and informative story."—*School Library Journal*

Also by Gloria Whelan

Small Acts of Amazing Courage

Chu Ju's House

Homeless Bird

Listening for Lions

Parade of Shadows

Angel on the Square

Goodbye Vietnam

The Summer of the War

ALL MY NOBLE
dreams
and then
WHAT HAPPENS

Gloria Whelan

A PAULA WISEMAN BOOK
SIMON & SCHUSTER BOOKS FOR YOUNG READERS
NEW YORK   LONDON   TORONTO   SYDNEY   NEW DELHI

SIMON & SCHUSTER BOOKS FOR YOUNG READERS
An imprint of Simon & Schuster Children's Publishing Division
1230 Avenue of the Americas, New York, New York 10020
This book is a work of fiction. Any references to historical events, real people, or real places are used fictitiously. Other names, characters, places, and events are products of the author's imagination, and any resemblance to actual events or places or persons, living or dead, is entirely coincidental.
Copyright © 2013 by Gloria Whelan
For information about special discounts for bulk purchases, please contact Simon & Schuster Special Sales at 1-866-506-1949 or business@simonandschuster.com.
The Simon & Schuster Speakers Bureau can bring authors to your live event. For more information or to book an event, contact the Simon & Schuster Speakers Bureau at 1-866-248-3049 or visit our website at www.simonspeakers.com.
Also available in a Simon & Schuster Books for Young Readers hardcover edition
Design by Lizzy Bromley
The text for this book is set in Bembo and Odette.
Manufactured in the United States of America, 0214 OFF
First Simon & Schuster Books for Young Readers paperback edition April 2014
2 4 6 8 10 9 7 5 3 1
The Library of Congress has cataloged the hardcover edition as follows:
Whelan, Gloria.
All my noble dreams and then what happens / Gloria Whelan.
p. cm.
"A Paula Wiseman Book."
Sequel to: Small acts of amazing courage.
Summary: As Rosalind continues to straddle the proper English world of her family and the culture of 1920s India where they live, her support of Gandhi and his followers in opposing British rule grows and she considers trying to carry the rebels' message to Edward, Prince of Wales, during his visit.
ISBN 978-1-4424-4976-3 (hc)
1. India—History—British occupation, 1765–1947—Juvenile fiction. [1. India—History—British occupation, 1765–1947—Fiction. 2. Insurgency—Fiction. 3. Family life—India—Fiction. 4. Aunts—Fiction. 5. Windsor, Edward, Duke of, 1894–1972—Fiction. 6. Great Britain—History—George V, 1910–1936—Fiction.] I. Title.
PZ7.W5718All 2013
[Fic]—dc23
2012018599
ISBN 978-1-4424-5157-5 (pbk)
ISBN 978-1-4424-4977-0 (eBook)

To Patricia and Thomas Brown

India, 1921

We live in India, but just as England won't let go of India, England has its hands on our family. You can tell a lot about that by what we have for breakfast. Father always manages to be at the table seconds before our cook, Gopel, has the food ready on the buffet. That way Father can start the day with a complaint. His breakfast is typically English: grilled kippers, eggs, bacon, and heaps of toast with Dundee marmalade. The marmalade comes to our home in India all the way from Scotland, and Father storms if we run out. After breakfast, he will leave for work. As deputy commissioner in the British Civil Service, his job is to tell the people of India what they must do, and because of the strike by the Indian people to protest England's rule, they may or may not do it.

Mother is not at breakfast. She is resting from the day before. She worries about everything, which exhausts her. She is arranged on her chaise longue, wearing a silk negligee trimmed in lace, her long gold hair falling over her shoulders, sipping the tea brought to her by Amina, who was once my *ayah* and is now Mother's lady's maid, since I no longer need a nursemaid. Mother will be choosing what to worry about today.

Aunt Ethyl, like Father, has an English breakfast. If she could wave a wand, she would turn India into England in a second. Gone would be the brightly colored parakeets, the mango and acacia trees, the bougainvilleas that weep blossoms like crimson and pink tears. Instead we would have England's gloomy skies, brown birds, and bare trees. She has been here in India for nearly two years, but on that morning, when the heat had already found its way into the house, she wore a well-starched, high-necked cotton blouse and a wool skirt, which covered every inch of her ankles like a gray cloud.

Aunt Louise is of two minds. She loves India, but she has not abandoned her native England. For breakfast she has *congee*, rice porridge. It is just what our Indian servants will be eating in the kitchen, but they will have spicy pickles with their *congee*. Aunt Louise, however, reaches for the toast and marmalade. Baneet, who has been tailor and dressmaker to our family forever, made for Aunt Louise a brightly colored blouse from some Indian cotton my aunt found in the bazaar. Her skirt, on the other hand, was of sturdy English serge. But here is the thing about Aunt Louise: While Aunt Ethyl's feet are imprisoned in tightly laced English oxfords, Aunt Louise goes about in sandals. The first morning she came down in a pair of sandals, Aunt Ethyl accused, "Louise, you are not fully dressed."

When I stayed with my aunts two years ago at their home in England, Aunt Ethyl was a terrible bully. She never tired of telling Aunt Louise what to do. I rescued Aunt Louise by taking her back to India with me, but Aunt Ethyl followed us as determined as a bloodhound, and here they were.

But this was the Aunt Louise of India, not England, for she had tucked a yellow hibiscus blossom in her hair. There was nothing in Aunt Ethyl's hair except long, sharp hairpins. The hairpins were to keep any tiny tendril of hair from escaping the tight knot Aunt Ethyl makes of her long

3

black hair. It's as if she was terrified someone might find her attractive.

As usual my breakfast was slapdash. I reached for whatever I could get down the fastest. When I finished, I would hurry to my tutor, Mr. Snartwell, then afterward to a forbidden place.

Something in the newspaper made Father roar like a lion. It was the strike, the *hartal*. Father's enemy, Mr. Gandhi, is a small man, half Father's size, but Gandhi is powerful. He is the head of the Indian National Congress, or the Congress Party, and he is leading the movement to free India from Great Britain's rule. The Congress Party had called for a *hartal*, a nonviolent strike to shut down all of India until England gives India her freedom. Indian students had left their British schools and colleges. Indians had boycotted the British courts and set up their own courts. They had left their jobs in railways and the police departments, which were all managed by us British. Gandhi was even calling for Indian soldiers to strike. This was especially infuriating to Father, who served in the Great War as a major in a battalion of the Gurkha Rifles. The men he commanded were Indian soldiers. Though the war ended in 1918, more than two years ago, Father was still an active officer in the British army, which had been called upon to keep order during the *hartal*.

Father cracked open his soft-boiled egg in a really brutal way. "The Indians are not ready for freedom," he said. "They spend all their money on festivals and marriages and funerals. One of their so-called holy beggars gets more respect than a good worker."

"Harlan," Aunt Louise said in a small voice, "surely we cannot criticize a man who has given up worldly goods to walk in the way of his religion."

"Nonsense," Aunt Ethyl said in a cross voice. "Who is to do that man's work?"

"They won't be taught," Father said. "They are half-starved. Why must it be just rice? Why don't they plant potatoes and eat them?"

"Why should we tell them what to eat?" I asked. A perfectly reasonable question. "And if they are half-starved, it's because of the pitiful wages we pay them." There was a time when I didn't care about such things, but then I met Max Nelson, who was a lieutenant in the British army and served under my father. Max went on to study history at Cambridge University, and now he's back here in India. It was Max who helped me see how unfair it is for England to rule over India. That means Father and I are always at war.

"Rosalind, you know nothing about these matters and had better stay with things you do know. Your meddling in the past has led you into predicaments that have been an embarrassment to us all."

"I'm sure Rosy did not mean any disrespect, Harlan," Aunt Louise said in her soft voice, "but surely there is something to be said for the longing of the Indian people for their independence." Aunt Louise, who spent years under the rule of Aunt Ethyl, understood what it was like to have someone always telling you what to do.

"They are no more than children," Aunt Ethyl said. "They would not know what to do with independence. They should be grateful to the British."

That was too much for me. "Civil disobedience and strikes are all that's left to the Indian people. They aren't allowed to make their own laws. England taxes them, tells them what they can write in their own newspapers, rules their courts, and tells them how they must live. Thousands of Indian soldiers died in the war to keep other countries free, only for the survivors to come back to their own country and have no freedom at all." I couldn't help saying what I thought. It was all so unfair.

Max would have been proud of me, but I knew I was in for it. Mercifully, Ranjit, our *burra mali*, the head of our household servants, came into the dining room and presented to Father the morning mail on a silver salver. It was Father's rule that the servants should see no unpleasantness among us, so my scolding was put off.

While Father went through the mail, Aunt Ethyl and Aunt Louise made plans for their day. They both volunteered at an orphanage for Indian children where my baby was. Well, not really my baby, but Nadi is there because of me. I was the one who rescued Nadi from an evil man who wanted to harm him. Two years ago I learned that our sweeper had lost his job and, because his family was starving, he had sold his grandson to Pandy. Pandy was a horrible man who twisted the arms and legs of babies so they would grow up to be pitiful sights. He put the deformed children about the streets of the bazaar as beggars. Much to Father's horror, I bought the baby from Pandy and gave him to Mrs. Nelson's orphanage.

Aunt Ethyl brought healthcare and proper British manners to the children at the orphanage. Aunt Louise told them stories, wiped their bottoms, and gave them hugs. The orphanage was the idea of Mrs. Nelson, who

7

is the wife of a very rich jute merchant. She is also the mother of Max, whom Father has forbidden me to see ever again. That's because Max and I got into trouble going to demonstrations here, and even in London, supporting Gandhi. We nearly ended up in jail. The thing is, I see Max nearly every day.

Using his knife, Father opened an envelope, getting egg on it. "I see your mother has been at the shops again." Father sighed deeply as he examined the bill. "Well, of course, there are parties and such, and she must have what she needs." After all these years, Father was still head over heels in love with Mother.

He looked carefully at the return address on a thick envelope in some rich, creamy stationary. His face turned red, and he quickly wiped the remaining egg from his knife, examining it carefully to be sure it was clean. Then, deliberately, as if he were a doctor opening someone's chest to get at his heart, Father opened the envelope and extracted a folded page made of the same heavy paper. We were all looking at him now, waiting for what was coming.

In wonder, as if he couldn't quite believe it, Father announced, "His Royal Highness, the Prince of Wales, will be coming to Calcutta in December. My battalion of the Gurkha Rifles is to be a part of the honor guard, and of course I will command it. Our family is invited to Calcutta for all the festivities." He was smiling now, all his earlier irritation gone. He was pleased to give us this gift, and he was full of pride at being a part of the Prince of Wales's visit.

"Oh, Harlan," Aunt Louise said, "what a great honor for you. And well deserved. I am so pleased. I have always been fond of the prince. He was a very sweet child, but mischievous. I recall hearing that as a little boy David disliked his governess so much he made a tadpole sandwich for her."

"Louise!" Aunt Ethyl was horrified. She regarded all the members of the royal family as gods. "What can you be thinking? How dare you refer to the prince as 'David'? And I am sure there can be no truth to such a rumor. She turned to Father. "The honor, Harlan, is very deserved."

"Ranjit," Father said, "will you ask the Memsahib to join us?" Ranjit swaggered a little as he left on his happy errand. I was sure he considered it a great honor to be a part of a household whose family would meet the prince. Ranjit would have nothing to do with Gandhi or the

Congress Party. Though an Indian, he is more British than Father is.

After Ranjit went in search of Mother, Father said, "There can be none of this *hartal* strike thing with the prince in this country. He will set things to rights."

I didn't say anything, but what I thought was that for Gandhi and the Congress Party, the presence on Indian soil of the son of the king who ruled over them would be a kind of punishment. It was like rubbing their noses in their hateful subjugation. One day the Prince of Wales, like his father, George V, would be Emperor of India. Mahatma Gandhi had spent his entire adult life working for the freedom for the Indian people. He objected to England making all the decisions about how the people of India lived. He had been in and out of jail, but he had never given up. The presence of a member of England's ruling family in his country would make Gandhi all the more determined to put an end to British rule. I couldn't wait to see Max and tell him the news, although he probably already knew, for he was working as a reporter for *Young India*, Gandhi's very own magazine. He founded the publication and still writes for it.

Of course, like Max, who cares so much for the fight

for India's freedom, I was also a supporter of Gandhi, but a little part of me was excited at the thought of meeting the Prince of Wales. I'd seen his picture. The twenty-eight-year-old prince was handsome, with lovely eyes, blond hair that fell over his forehead, and a rather sad look that made you want to cheer him up. I would never let Max know, but I was quite looking forward to seeing His Royal Highness. I wondered how close I would get.

Father said, "The prince served very credibly with the British armed forces in the war. He was a brave chap, wanting to fight on the front, but the generals forbade it, afraid he might be kidnapped by the enemy and held for ransom. It is a great honor for India to have him visit."

Mother swept into the room, so excited, the lace collar on her negligee seemed to stand at attention. All her usual morning languor was gone. "Harlan, what marvelous news. I am delighted for you. What an honor. I must get busy at once. If we're to attend receptions and teas, we will all need clothes. Ethyl and Louise, I count on you to help. We must choose fabric for our dresses at once and get in Baneet to do the sewing before the other families get to him."

Father looked alarmed. He was probably thinking of the bill that had come in the morning's mail. "I hope,

Cecelia, you will not overdo it. You won't want a closet of frocks you will never wear again."

"Harlan, you can't want your family to disgrace you. If you've been awarded this position of honor, of course we must do you proud. You wouldn't have us go before the Prince of Wales in rags."

"Oh, I say, Cecelia, that's not fair. Of course you must have what's proper, but within reason."

Aunt Ethyl said, "I am sure there is something in my trunk from England that would do very well, and, Louise, you have your brown velvet." It troubled Aunt Ethyl to spend even a penny.

"Ethyl," Mother said, "velvet in India's heat? Impossible. It would be like wearing a fur coat. For once you must let me organize something elegant. Rosalind, you must have a new formal dress. You've grown so your old one is above your ankles. Tomorrow you must go into the bazaar with me. You know the way around there, and I always get lost. I have heard there is a stall with lovely silks. Today I'm off to the club. There was a new issue of *The Queen* there yesterday with all the latest fashions from London. I must get my hands on it."

And away Mother went, full of energy, as if all the lying

on her chaise longue was just to rest up for something like this.

Father pushed his chair from the table with so much energy it skated halfway across the tile floor. "Well, we must all carry on."

Before leaving, I asked my aunts how Nadi was. Father was strict about my not spending time with Nadi, but I missed him and regretted not seeing all the little changes that must have been happening.

Aunt Ethyl said, "Nadi is doing very well, my dear. I believe I have him successfully trained for the potty. There was a little accident yesterday, but I had a serious talk with him. One has to be quite strict about such things."

Aunt Louise laughed. "Ethyl, I am sure that is the last thing Rosy wants to hear about. The child is blooming. I taught him a song, and of course he doesn't know all the words, but he burbles on quite in tune. We have a new game we play. Nadi toddles off and hides, and I make a great thing about finding him."

"I don't think you should play that after meals, Louise," Aunt Ethyl said. "It keeps the child's food from settling properly."

I was anxious to be off and didn't want to be in the

middle of one of their little disagreements. Giving them a kiss and hug, I told them what an excellent job they were doing at the orphanage and hurried away to do one thing I should and one thing I shouldn't.

2

The way to my tutor took me along the river, which is the heart of our village. Women in their bright *saris* perched along the shore like colorful birds. They gossiped as they washed the family laundry, scraping the clothes against the stones. The fishing boats had sailed out with the dawn. Men too old to fish were left behind to mend the nets.

Ships carrying jute from plantations upriver were tied along the docks to be unloaded. The bundles of jute balanced on the heads of the bearers weighed more than the men who carried them. The great tangles and snakes of jute would be cleaned, graded, and pressed into bales and sent by steamer to mills in Calcutta. With all that jute, I thought, you could make enough rope to tie the whole world into a neat package.

I once asked Max if he wanted to go into his father's jute business. "It's the last thing in the world I would want to do," he said. I think the more he saw of the world, the larger his ideas grew. I was sure he would never be content to settle down in his father's factory. Still, I didn't think he should forget where the money for the orphanage came from.

"It's the money made by your father's jute that supports your mother's orphanage."

"When I have helped Gandhi to make India free," Max said, "the Indian people will own their own jute factories and there will be no need for orphanages."

"England is free, and there are orphanages there."

But Max didn't pay a lot of attention to my arguments, considering them not as informed as his superior knowledge.

I left the river and biked past the cantonment where the army is quartered and past the *maidan* where parades and meetings take place. It was where Max and I were arrested for going to hear Gandhi speak two years ago. My arrest angered Father so much he sent me off to England to live with my aunts. But Father didn't know that Max would be in England, too, completing his studies at Cambridge University. One night, he talked Aunt Louise and me into going with him to a meeting with a supporter of Gandhi. Little did we know that our pictures at the meeting would appear in the newspaper the next day! Although Father never learned about the pictures, I was sent back to India for he saw how unhappy Mother was to have me so far away.

I parked my bike in front of one of several well-kept homes where many of the British civil servants lived. Mr. Snartwell is not a civil servant, but his father had been the budget director of our town and the house had once belonged to him. As a young boy Mr. Snartwell was sent off to England to be educated in British schools. He received honors at Oxford University, and great things were expected of him when he returned to India, but he would have nothing to do with government service. He was a great disappointment to his parents, who had long since died. Mr. Snartwell stayed on in India with his wife, Wilfreda. He writes long books about obscure English poets. I know not a single soul who has read one of his

17

books, but on his wall are framed certificates of honors he received from the British Royal Academy, so someone is reading them—someone important.

After I returned from England, I was too old to return to my old school. Because Mr. Snartwell is such a scholar, Father sends me each day to be tutored by him in English literature. "I won't have you growing up, Rosalind, with no knowledge of England's great literary tradition. Besides, listening to Snartwell will help you to improve your enunciation."

Father is a great admirer of Shakespeare, and I sometimes hear him in the garden, when he thinks no one is listening, declaiming

> *To be, or not to be: that is the question:*
> *Whether 'tis nobler in the mind to suffer*
> *The slings and arrows of outrageous fortune,*
> *Or to take arms against a sea of troubles*
> *And by opposing end them?*

Father is no Hamlet, and you just know he wouldn't have any trouble making a decision to take up arms.

Father worries that I spend too much time with my friend Isha chattering in Hindi. Isha is the daughter of my former nursemaid, Amina. Isha and I grew up together, and she is a dear friend of mine. She learned English from me, and I learned Hindi from her.

I have an agreement with Mr. Snartwell. Instead of the four hours Father has arranged for me to be tutored, I am there for two hours. That gives me time for my secret project, and it leaves Mr. Snartwell at peace to write his next learned book. I am sure money is scarce in the Snartwell household, most of it going for ink and the piles of paper I see in my tutor's study. Even the little money Father pays would be welcome; otherwise, how to account for the poor man putting up with my ignorance?

Mrs. Snartwell is a mouse of a woman scurrying about to make everything pleasant for her husband. Every time I see her, she is wearing the same dress, her red hair swept severely back so that its natural curl is checked.

She always greets me with great friendliness, inquiring about Mother and Father and my aunts, none of whom she has ever met, for her husband is only a scholar and not one of the civil servants who govern India. She doesn't come to the club for bridge afternoons, and you don't see the Snartwells at club dances. The club has no use for scholars. Even if they did, she could not appear in a shabby housedress.

She made the usual excuse for not offering me biscuits with my tea. "My dear, I do apologize for not having a little treat for you, but I haven't had time to do the shopping." I knew well, however, that it was want of money and not want of time that kept her from shopping.

I was full of news. "The Prince of Wales is coming to Calcutta," I told her. "Our whole family is going there for the ceremonies."

"Oh, what an experience that will be for you." Her eyes grew large, and there was a dreamy look on her face. "I suppose you will attend all the teas and the formal ball. Just imagine. You must promise to tell me all about it. How I should love to see the prince."

There was no chance of that. I couldn't imagine Mrs. Snartwell in her housedress amidst all the finery of a royal ball. I wished I could wave a wand and make it possible.

Mr. Snartwell put his book aside and looked up as from a very long distance. "Ah, Miss James. Is it time for your lesson already?" Regretfully, he closed his book and arranged a smile of welcome that convinced neither of us. "What have you chosen for today's session?"

I have a thick book of English poetry, and from time to time Mr. Snartwell allows me to memorize something

I choose myself. I have been reading *The Rubaiyat of Omar Khayyam*. It's a love poem written by a Persian poet long ago and translated by a Mr. FitzGerald who lived for many years right here in India. It's so sad, you can't help but love it. With great feeling I recited,

> *Yon rising Moon that looks for us again—*
> *How oft hereafter will she wax and wane;*
> *How oft hereafter rising look for us*
> *Through this same Garden—*
>   *and for one in vain!*

I was nearly in tears thinking about the lover who had gone away. Mr. Snartwell said, "That's a very pretty bit, Rosalind, but if it is love lyrics you want, I have something better." And he traveled about the room searching the bookshelves that lined the walls of his study. I was sure he had every book ever written, and I was also sure that all the pretty dresses Mrs. Snartwell might have had and even the food the Snartwells might have eaten were stacked there on the shelves.

"Ah, here it is. *The Sonnets of Shakespeare*." In his dry voice he read,

Gloria Whelan

Shall I compare thee to a summer's day?
Thou art more lovely and more temperate:

"Those words, Rosalind, have much beauty and none of the sentimentality of Mr. FitzGerald's efforts."

I read the poem, and it was very beautiful, but then we spent the next hours dissecting its sonnet form and studying how iambic pentameter differs from iambic hexameter and something called hendecasyllables and after a while, I hated the poem. I couldn't hide from my tutor that I was bored. He bid me farewell and sent me on my way with a regretful look like someone releasing at last into freedom a bird he had tried in vain to tame.

October was my favorite month. Gone were the monsoon rains that turned the world green with mold and carried the river mud into the streets. The morning air was almost cool. I left the British section of town and headed for the tiny shacks where the Indians make their homes. There, beneath an enormous bo tree, I saw a few small boys waving frantically to me. Like Mr. Snartwell, I had students.

Mr. Gandhi's *hartal* had closed the schools run by the British for Indian students; even the mission schools were boycotted by the Indian National Congress. Max, who had more faith in my teaching ability than I had and who was always getting me to do more than I believed I could, convinced several Indian families that I was on their side and that my school was not an official British school. At first the fathers were horrified by the idea of a girl teaching their sons, but they were anxious for the boys to learn, and mine was the only unofficial school offered in this part of town. I got on well with the boys. My class was limited to simple mathematics, which had its own language, and English, which every child who wants to get on in British India must know, for the British will not learn Hindi.

My father would have been furious if he'd known of the school. First of all, I am helping out the strike, and then I am in the Indian section of town. Worst of all, he would think I was wasting great English literature on children whom he believed would grow up to have no better job than the carrying of jute bundles on their heads. But if all the while you were carrying the bundles you could say to yourself Shakespeare's words, as my father does, the carrying would not be so heavy. What would really surprise Father is that I also teach great writers in the Indian language, like the poet Tagore, who is my favorite. Max has taught me his poems, like the one where Tagore describes how stars talk to him and the one where he says days and nights pass and bloom and fade like flowers.

The boys crowded around me. Manu put a bouquet of jasmine on my desk. Bimal brought me the gift of a tiny green lizard. Dev told me he wanted to be Antony, who gets to kill Caesar in the Shakespeare play we were acting out. Goral wanted to be Caesar. "He got killed, but he was the most famous."

I shepherded them into the classroom. The room, with its metal roof, had been shut up since the day before and was suffocating. I flung open the windows and left the door open so mosquitoes and flies could join our class. A little parade of stag beetles started to march out the door, but Dev begged for my handkerchief and used it to imprison them. Later the boys would have races with the beetles.

When everyone had settled down, I explained how Caesar was considered by some to be a tyrant. Antony and the men who killed him wanted freedom. "The killing was evil," I told the boys, and talked to them about Gandhi and the *hartal*. I explained that Gandhi believed that nonviolence had a greater effect than the force of arms. "'Nonviolence,' he said, 'is the greatest force at the disposal of mankind.'" But my fine talk bored them. The day was warm, and they were watching a monkey up in the bo tree. They didn't want a lecture about freedom. They wanted the play.

Bimal and Goral had wheedled their sisters' old saris, and we looked at pictures I had brought to guide us in the making of roman togas. Ishat ran out for leaves from the bo tree, and we made a laurel crown for Caesar. While all of this was going on, I saw a figure lingering just outside. When I started for the window to see who was spying on us, wondering if I was going to get into trouble, Dev said, "It's only my sister, Sajala."

"What is she doing outside the school?"

"The stupid girl thinks she can learn by listening to us. She leaves the sorting of the lentils for my mother and sneaks off, pretending she is at the river washing clothes."

"She must come inside and be part of the class." When I began the school, I was disappointed that there were no girls.

The boys were in an uproar. Even little Manu, who sat through his lessons gazing at me with worshipful eyes, was indignant. "Girls aren't allowed in school," he said.

"Nonsense. She can be Caesar's wife in our play." I

was angry and went in search of Sajala, who had heard the whole thing and was crouched by the wall, too frightened to move. Her hands were clenched into fists, and even her braid seemed to cower.

"Don't be frightened, Sajala, you can come into the school."

"No, no. The boys will hate me and run away."

I pried loose one of her fists and, taking her hand, coaxed her into the classroom, whereupon all the boys howled and, pushing past us, disappeared. I didn't know if I should take a stand. Even if I could persuade Sajala to come to my school, it would be a school of only one and all the boys would lose their opportunity to learn. But to give in would be against my principles. I decided on a compromise. "Sajala," I said, "wait by the window and listen like you were doing, and I'll stay after school for a half hour to help you with the lesson."

She put the tip of her braid in her mouth and sucked at it, which I learned later was a sign of happiness. When I walked into the classroom without Sajala, the boys who had been sitting in the branches of the bo tree hopped down and followed me in. They wanted to celebrate their victory, but when they saw the expression on my face and the way I was slashing away at their arithmetic homework, awarding low marks to everyone, they settled in to their seats without a word. To punish them and to make myself feel better for giving in, I said, "We will do the play tomorrow." Dev and Goral gave me disappointed looks.

I smelled the fragrance of Manu's bouquet of jasmine on my desk and let Bimel's little green lizard crawl up my arm. Its tiny sticky feet were strangely comforting. "I'll bring tomato sauce tomorrow for the blood," I said, and everyone was happy again.

After school was over, I found Sajala. At thirteen or fourteen, she was older than the boys in class. I was surprised to see her sari was made from *khadi*. Her family, I decided, must be followers of Gandhi. Gandhi had asked all the Indians to boycott British cotton and to spin thread to make into their own cloth, which they called *khadi*. The British bought Indian cotton at low prices, then shipped it to England, where the cotton was made into cloth in British mills and sent back to India for the Indians to buy at a high price. Gandhi believed that if Indians spun their own thread, and made their own cloth, it would put people to work, and it would keep England from making money from their labor.

"Does your mother spin thread?" I asked Sajala.

"Yes, I can spin also, but there is more I want to learn."

"What is it you want to learn at our school?

"What you teach my brother."

"Do you know any arithmetic?" I asked.

Sajala gave me a puzzled look.

"Do you go to the bazaar for your mother?" She nodded. "Do you buy spices and lentils for her?" Another nod. "Do you pay *annas* for what you buy and count the change to be sure you haven't been cheated?" A vigorous nod.

"Then you know addition and subtraction," I told her. Today we'll talk about multiplication. Suppose you know how many mangos there are on one tree and how many mango trees you have, you can find out nearly how many mangos you have altogether without counting each one." Sajala was so eager to learn that the half hour went quickly. All the while, Dev was watching from behind the bo tree. When Sajala left for home, he trotted beside her. "Multiplication is baby stuff," he told her. "I know how to divide, even long numbers."

Sajala didn't care. She walked along sucking her braid in a happy way.

3

On the way home I stopped to see Isha. I was hungry and there was always something good to eat and plenty of excitement at the home of Isha's in-laws. Isha was Amina's daughter. When Amina was my *ayah* she would bring Isha along with her to play with me. Mother's friends said, "How can you allow your daughter to play with an Indian child?" Mother could not bear to separate a mother from her child. Her own child, my brother Edward, was sent to school in England and died there. Mother has never recovered from his death. It follows her like a shadow on even the sunniest days and sends her to her chaise longue to mourn.

As was customary, Isha married at a young age. Three years ago, when she was only fifteen, she married Aziz Mertha and learned all about marriage. Isha, as was usual, lived in the home of Aziz's parents. At first Isha's *sass*, her mother-in-law, made life miserable for her, but since she had a baby and the baby is a boy, all is well. Eka was walking now and stood beside Isha, hanging on to her sari with both hands. He was a cheerful boy and smiled at everything: people, dogs, lizards, and cockroaches.

Isha gave me the greatest gift of all. She gave me India. With Isha I learned Hindi. It was at her home I first ate *poppadums* and *khichdi*. She showed me the magic of the bazaar, where you can buy paper kites or gold bracelets. In return I gave her English, and British customs to marvel and laugh at.

"Rosy," Isha looked up from the *chapati* she was slapping into shape. "Every day there is a new crisis. The Congress Party told Aziz to close his stall in the bazaar for the *hartal*, but if he does, we will starve."

"And will he do it?"

"He does what Gandhiji and the Congress Party say to do. 'Isha,' he says, 'I am ashamed to make money when poorer men than I are willing to starve for the sake of freedom.' I asked him, 'Can you buy a kilo of lentils with freedom?'"

"What do Aziz's mother and father say?"

"They care little for talk of freedom, but Aziz is the oldest son. They give in to him in everything. If I criticize the Congress Party, they say I am a *jinn*, an evil spirit, and threaten to take Eka from me and send me away. Of course they don't mean it, but every time Aziz goes to one of his secret Congress meetings, I take Eka and hide in our room, waiting for the police."

But Isha can't be unhappy for more than a moment. In her next breath she said, "My *sass* has given me one of her best saris."

Isha hurried into her room and returned draped in a sari of the finest muslin the color of peaches. I knew there was only one thing that would make Isha's sass give such a gift to her. "Isha, you're pregnant!"

"Yes, you guessed." She handed me a *chapati*, hot and crisp from the *chula* and slathered with *ghee*. "Yesterday I pretended I was a little sick and my sass made me stop work and lie down on my *charpoy*. All day I had to do nothing but play with Eka and read the English magazines you bring me. I like to read about your king and queen

31

and all the nobles: the duke of this and that and the earl of that and this. Why don't the British let us have our own dukes and earls to read about? You even have to send your prince over here to strut up and down in our country like a peacock."

"Isha!" I was angry with England for not giving India its freedom, but I had to admit there was a little of my father in me that was shocked to hear His Royal Highness called a peacock. "Our whole family is going to Calcutta to welcome the prince, and we're going to parties for him."

"Aziz and the Congress Party are also planning a welcome for him. They want to close down the city of Calcutta when the prince lands there." Then Isha's voice softened. "Ah, Rosy, you are lucky. I would give anything to go to such parties and see the peacock and all the fine clothes. Will you have a new frock?"

Now I was reluctant. Max treated British royalty much like Isha did. "I'm not sure I should go to such parties. I'm afraid to tell Max. He will be angry. Or, worse, he will laugh at me."

"What do you care?"

Then we forgot our talk of politics, and Isha brought out the old copies of *The Queen* I had given to her, which she had to hide from Aziz, who called such magazines "the leavings of a decadent empire and the foolishness of our enemy." Together Isha and I looked at dresses and talked of silks. "Look at this," Isha said, "the waistline is all the way down to the belly button!"

"And look at this dress. It's inches above the ankles!"

Suddenly, Isha pushed away the magazines. "I didn't want to say anything, but, Rosy, I must tell you. There is trouble for you."

"What do you mean?"

"Jetha has died."

It was Jetha who was fired by my father because he was too old and infirm to be our sweeper any longer. The sweeper and his family were sent away from our house and fell on hard times. To find money, Jetha sold his baby grandson to the cruel man Pandy. Pandy was the man who twisted the arms and legs of babies so they would grow into misshapen children to be put out into the bazaar to make people pity them and give money. How could I feel sorry that someone who could sell his grandchild to Pandy was gone? "But how does Jetha's death make trouble for me?"

"You don't understand," Isha said. "Now that Jetha is

dead, Jetha's son Iravat and Iravat's wife want their son back. Iravat has found work, and there will be food for Nadi."

"They can't have him! He's mine." And he was. I bought him from Pandy for a shilling to keep him from Pandy's cruelty. I gave him his name, Nadi, and took him to Mrs. Nelson's orphanage, where my aunts and everyone else there dotes on him and where you never see him without a smile on his face. It was impossible to think of him in Iravat's miserable shack, made to live as untouchables as Iravat and his family lived. The untouchables were the lowest of the low in Indian society. They had to do the most demeaning work: sweeping streets, carrying away dead animals, and cleaning latrines and sewers. They were forbidden in temples and schools. People would cross the street so even the shadow of an untouchable would not fall on them. How could I return Nadi to such a life?

In the past when I complained of the life of the untouchables to Isha, all she said was, "That is their *karma*." Now I accused her, "You told me to buy the baby. You said to give my shilling for Nadi." How could I forget that horrible trip under the bridge where Pandy and the other thieves lived, those angry eyes staring at me in the dark and that evil Pandy, whose hand I had to touch when I gave him the shilling for Nadi? "They let Jetha sell their baby. Why should I have to give Nadi back?"

Isha said, "You have never starved. You don't know what sadness people are driven to."

I believed Isha was pleading for the mother and father because she was pregnant and carrying her own baby. I was uncertain, but only for a moment. "I'll never let them have the child," I said. "If I have to, I'll steal him from the orphanage." As soon as I said the word "orphanage" I worried that his parents already had their hands on Nadi. I snatched another *chapati*, got onto my bicycle, and pedaled away as fast as I could. I just wanted to get my arms around Nadi and hold him so tightly no one could take him away. I had dreams and ambitions for Nadi. He would grow up to become a great leader of his people, a disciple of Gandhi who would carry on Gandhi's fight for India's freedom. Nadi would certainly never be an untouchable, shut into a world of "don't" and "forbidden" and "unworthy."

The orphanage had once been a jute *godown*, a warehouse, and was now transformed into dormitories and classrooms. It was a pleasant place surrounded by gardens. In the gardens a dozen Indian children were playing a game with a young

Indian employee of the orphanage. I looked for Nadi, but at this time of day he would be having his nap in the cool dormitory with its little *charpoys* and clean sheets. He would not be in some dirty hovel with a mud floor and bugs crawling about.

I found my aunts and Mrs. Nelson in the kitchen, going over the menu for the next day, making lists of what must be purchased. Aunt Louise wanted the treat of *hawla* for the children who loved sweetmeats, but Aunt Ethyl spoke of toothaches and stomachaches.

Mrs. Nelson looked up. "Rosalind, my dear, what is it? You look as if you had a terrible fright. What happened, my dear?"

All my worries over Nadi came in a tumble of words.

For once Aunt Ethyl and I were on the same side. "Impossible," she said. "You could not send a child back to such parents. They would not boil the child's water, and they would not wash his vegetables in a proper disinfectant. The poor child might get dysentery, cholera, even leprosy!"

Aunt Louise's response shocked me. She said, "What must that mother have suffered to see her baby stolen from her by her wicked father-in-law, and now to know he is being raised only a short distance from her by strangers."

I turned to Mrs. Nelson, whom I was sure would side with me. She would never allow Nadi to go from her orphanage, where he was safe and well cared for.

"Sit down, Rosalind, and have some lemonade. You are all in a tangle." She handed me a cool glass, and I gulped down the bittersweet drink. "I have known about this for some time, but I haven't mentioned it. I wanted to wait until I knew in my own heart what was best for Nadi."

"There can't be any question, Mrs. Nelson. Nadi is happy and well here. He has a home with good food and people like you and my aunts and all the Indian women who work here and who love him."

"We love him, but none of us is his mother or his father."

"But they were terrible parents. They don't deserve him."

"Rosalind." There was an unaccustomed frown on her face. "You can't know that. You've never faced starvation for the lack of a few grains of rice. Nadi's mother had to think not only of Nadi but of her other children as well."

At that moment Max appeared. "I saw your bike outside, Rosy. What's the matter? You look like you've been chased by demons. Certainly you don't look like the young lady who will dance with the Prince of Wales. Your father's honor and your family's visit to Calcutta are the talk of the town."

"Max, don't tease. This is deadly serious. Iravat now has a job and his wicked father has died, and they want Nadi back, and I can't make your mother or Aunt Louise understand how wrong that is. You've got to help me convince them it would be the worst thing in the world for Nadi. His family will just sell him all over again."

"Then you must buy him again."

Mrs. Nelson said, "Max, this is a serious matter. We don't need your frivolous ideas."

I didn't think it was a frivolous idea at all. It made perfect sense to me. I had a little money of my own that Father had given me for my birthday months ago. It was for a new dress, but I had never gotten around to having one made. I would go to Nadi's parents. I would offer to buy Nadi again, and when they agreed and took the money, as I was certain they would, I would be vindicated. I would show Isha and Aunt Louise and Mrs. Nelson how wrong they were. They would see that all Nadi's mother cared about was money.

Before anyone could say another word, I was running for the door. I heard Mrs. Nelson and my aunts calling me back. Max followed me outside. "Rosy." He put a hand on my shoulder. I could tell from the serious look on his face that I was in for a lecture. "I apologize. I didn't mean to make light of Nadi going back to his parents, but just think for a minute like his parents and not like a British girl."

I shut my ears, this time refusing to listen to Max. I pulled away, and in seconds I was on my bike and cycling toward the section at the outskirts of the city set aside for the untouchables, where I would find Nadi's parents. It was a part of our city most British never see. The untouchables were forbidden to live with Indians of caste. Their cast told Indians what their life would be like and whom they might take as friends. There was no caste for the untouchables. They were cast out. The words "cast out" were terrible, so final, so hopeless, and now people were saying that was to be Nadi's life.

In the untouchable village the only landscaping was mud. I saw no green thing, no trees or flowers or anything pleasant to the eye. It was as if all the beauty of the countryside had been cast out as well. The huts were fashioned of mud so that they looked like they had grown from the earth. The roofs were covered with bamboo. The earthen walls would melt with the first monsoon. The children and elders who were not working squatted outside their hut. Like the children at the orphanage, there were children running about laughing. In front of one hut a woman sat with a baby in her arms, singing to the child in a soft, melodious voice some Indian lullaby. I went to her, and she drew quickly apart from me as if she wished to protect me from any contact with her.

"Please, could you tell me where Iravat's wife is?" Alarmed by how I was bending close, the better to speak to her, she drew her *sari* across her face to further separate us.

"Memsahib, Iravat's wife has taken her children to the river for their washing."

I thanked her. As I hurried away I sensed her eyes following me—thinking, no doubt, that I, a British Memsahib, was mad to be there in that forbidden place.

I knew at what part of the river Iravat's wife would be. Untouchables must be downstream so no part of the water that touched them would flow past others who might be bathing. There was a muddy bit of the river allowed to the untouchables. It was in a mangrove swamp with its tangle of roots growing above the water like a puzzle.

I recognized Safia, Iravat's wife and Nadi's mother. Until this moment I had forgotten that when I was very little and she was just a young girl, Safia would come to bring Jetha a bit of rice for his supper. I remembered her graceful figure slipping like a shadow through the trees and shrubbery to find her *sassur* at his tasks of sweeping clear the paths in the garden.

She must have known me as well, for with a frightened look she called to two little boys, four or five years old. I was startled when I saw how much they looked like Nadi. She held on to them as if I were there to steal them. Putting her hands together and bowing very low, she made a *namaste*, a greeting of respect. In my best Hindi I said, "I'm here to give you something. I have money at home. You can have it if you promise not to take Nadi away from the orphanage." I expected a smile at the mention of money; instead Safia began to cry. "No, no. Not money. We have food now. I want my son."

I was angry at the refusal, and impatient. I was sure she only wanted more money. "You sold your son."

"I didn't want to do it. When your father fired him, my *sassur* said we were starving and there was no food for him and for Iravat and my boys. He said we would all die.

41

I promised to eat the grass in the field. I wanted nothing, only that he should not sell my boy to that evil man. I cried and cried. My *sassur* hit me and bound me so I was helpless. Now the old man is dead. Jetha has a job. We have enough food to feed our son."

Thinking of the starving family and of Safia being beaten and her son taken from her, I became less certain. "He is well cared for," I said. "Everyone at the orphanage loves him."

"How can they love him like I do?"

"At the orphanage there is good food, and it's so nice and clean."

"I tell you we have food now. Come and see our house. I am a good housekeeper." Scooping up a child in either arm, Safia ran ahead of me, less frightened now, almost happy, as if she believed it was all a matter of a clean house.

The woman with the baby was still there, but seeing Safia hurrying with a child under each arm, the woman quickly disappeared into her hut as if I were some *jinn* meant to do them all harm. Safia pointed to one of the huts. It did look a little more solid than the others, with a window cut out on either side. The roof was a sheet of metal. In front of the entry a single marigold sported a tired

42

bloom of a faint orange. Safia motioned me inside. She was so eager to show off the hut that she forgot about having to keep her distance and grabbed at my sleeve to pull me inside. Then, realizing what she had done, she crushed her body against the wall to keep herself from touching me.

"Safia"—I put my hand on her arm—"I'm not afraid of you. I want to be your friend."

She repeated the word "friend" in a puzzled tone, as if it could have no meaning between us. But then, recalling why I was there, she said, "See how clean, as good as the orphanage. I sweep the floor every day. And see." She showed me quilts used for bedding. They were neatly folded and cleverly made from brightly colored scraps of this and that.

When she saw me admiring the quilts, she said, "I sewed them myself." One of her little boys, understanding something of what his mother was doing, pulled at a fan fashioned from a bamboo leaf. He fanned himself with it and smiled at me, wanting me to see that there was even more in the house to be proud of. There was a tree stump that had been hollowed by years of pounding with a pestle. The hollow was golden from the spices used to make curries: coriander, tamarind, ginger, and cardamom.

I didn't want to see any of this. I wanted to keep the image in my head of slovenly misery. I made one more shameful attempt. "Are you sure I could not give you money for Nadi?"

"Who is this Nadi?"

"That's what we call your son."

"That is not my son's name. He is called Hari."

So he would lose even his name.

"I will not sell my son like my *sassur* did."

"What of your husband, Iravat?" I asked, eager to get around her. Perhaps so that I might bribe Iravat? There was no end to my selfishness.

Then I saw her hurt look, and at last I crept away thinking of William, the husband of Mrs. Blodget, the woman who had accompanied me on my voyage to England. Her husband had long since died, but she told me that whenever she was in doubt, William always whispered in her ear, telling her the right thing to do. All the way home I told myself that Nadi must stay in the orphanage and be safe, and all the way home Safia's look of rebuke followed me.

Later, when I confided to Max what had happened, I pleaded, "I meant well."

"Rosy, you did a brave thing when you rescued Nadi

from that evil Pandy, but you can't rescue every Indian child whose mother and father are poor. If that is the criterion, you will have millions sharing your house and your dinner. Put yourself in the place of Nadi's family. First they had to endure the sale of their son, and then the thought that he would have the horrible fate of children mutilated to be beggars. The alternative was to let their other children starve. Think how Nadi's mother would long to have her son back in her arms. The solution isn't to keep Nadi from his parents. The solution is to change the life of the untouchables."

I knew that Max was right. Max was like William. He told me the right thing to do. Why was the right thing to do always the hardest thing?

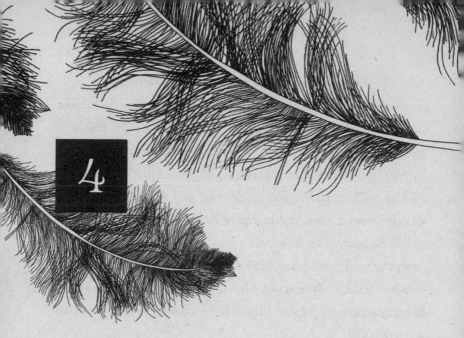

4

The next week, Iravat and Safia came to the orphanage for their son, and Mrs. Nelson gave Nadi to his parents. Mrs. Nelson forbade me to be there, worried there would be a flood of tears. Aunt Ethyl was forbidden as well, for fear she would grab Nadi from the arms of his mother and carry him off to England. Mrs. Nelson told me Nadi's parents would be happy to have me visit Nadi, that they were ashamed of having sold him and grateful to me for rescuing him.

Mother tried to comfort me. "Rosalind, dear, it was a brave, unselfish thing you did when you rescued Nadi from that terrible man, but this is even more brave and more unselfish." I knew Mother was thinking of my brother Edward and how she had lost him. Why would she not want a mother to be reunited with her son?

Mother and my aunts were soon caught up in preparations for the parties that would be held during the prince's visit. I hadn't the heart to shop for fancy clothes, and Mother and my aunts went alone to the bazaar. When they had returned, Aunt Louise said, "Rosy, we have chosen a blue for your dress just the color of your eyes. The prince will be dazzled."

"Don't put foolish ideas into the child's head," Aunt Ethyl said. "The festivities are to honor His Royal Highness the Prince of Wales, not to dazzle him, and there is little chance Rosalind will get close enough for the prince to see the color of her eyes."

I had to be dragged into the house from the garden, where I was sulking with a book under a mango tree, and made to stand still while Baneet stuck pins in me and complained about my lack of bosom. "I will fill it in with pleats and a frill," he said.

Isha laughed when I told her. "You should be married and have babies like I have. Then you would fill out your blouse." She wanted to hear all about my dress, and see a sample of the silk. Amina had described my mother's dress and Isha begged to see that as well. Secretly, we sneaked into the sewing room, and Isha passed judgment. "Your mother will be the loveliest woman at the ball." We giggled together at the thought of the prince falling madly in love with Mother, for I had told Isha the gossip at the club about the prince's preference for married ladies.

With Mr. Snartwell's tutoring and my little school, there wasn't much time for the club, which I had always considered the most boring place in the world. Amy Weston and Sarah Harvey were the only girls there who were my age. Amy and Sarah had always considered me odd, what with my visits to the bazaar and my friendship with Isha. I wasn't *pukka*. I wasn't what a well-bred English girl should be. I had slipped too much into the country in which I lived. I had forgotten that nothing mattered more than upholding British traditions.

Their attitude toward me changed when it became known that Father would be a part of the honor guard in Calcutta for the prince's visit and that our family would be invited to the festivities. Unlike Amy and Sarah, I was going to meet the prince. They were livid with jealousy, which they attempted to hide as they tried to wheedle information from me about the parties.

Sarah said she had a picture of the prince in his uniform tacked up over her bed, and Amy could rattle off all his names: Edward Albert Christian George Andrew Patrick David Windsor. Since I had suffered their snobbishness for years, I enjoyed taunting them with absurd stories. "Mother and I and my aunts are going to the parties in a special coach pulled by six white horses. It will be right behind the viceroy's coach. The prince will be reviewing the troops with Father, so Father has promised to ask the prince to dance at least one dance with me." Of course none of it was true. Father would cut off his head with his own sword before he did anything of the kind, but Sarah and Amy were so full of prince worship they believed every foolish thing I said. For the first time in my life, Sarah and Amy actually sought me out instead of exchanging looks of boredom when they saw me coming.

I was just back from a late afternoon at the club and a happy hour of describing to Sarah and Amy how I was to have my grandmother's diamond earrings to wear to the formal ball, when in truth Mother once told me her mother had tender ears and never wore earrings. I was feeling pleasantly smug when Isha stopped me at the door to our house. She was out of breath, and a tail of her *sari* was dragging in the grass. "Rosy, it is the end of the world! Your British are after the Congress Party, and they have put my Aziz into jail."

"What do you mean?"

"There was a meeting of the Congress Party last night. The word has gone out from Gandhi that your prince must see how strongly our country desires its freedom from his country so that he will take the message back to his father, the king. Gandhi says everything must be shut down for your prince's visit to Calcutta. The leaders of the Congress Party in our town were planning how that could be done. Someone told the British of the meeting, and they sent the police to arrest everyone there, and Aziz with them. The police came to our house and frightened my little boy, Eka. My mother begged your mother to speak to your father, but your mother does not like to hear hard things and is not someone who will fight for Aziz."

I knew that was true. I could never recall a time when Mother did not give in to Father. "Isha, what are you going to do?"

"It's what *you* can do."

50

"What do you mean? Is there going to be a demonstration for their freedom? Of course I will come."

"What good is a demonstration? The police will only arrest all the demonstrators until the whole country is in jail. You must talk with your father."

"Isha, you know my father. He's against the Congress Party. He despises Gandhi. He won't lift a finger for Aziz."

"Then you must find a way to make him. Now I must go to the jail and take Aziz some food. The leaders of the Congress Party are well treated and have their own rooms. Your British know that if it were otherwise, they would make a fuss, if they don't, but men like Aziz are considered of little worth, and they are all crowded into a small room and not given enough food to keep them alive."

Isha's voice was cold, and I felt for the first time in my life like the enemy. "Isha, listen. You know I am on your side in this."

"Then get your father to let my Aziz go." Her voice was only slightly warmer, and I knew our friendship as well as Aziz's freedom was at stake. I would mourn Aziz's imprisonment, but I would die without Isha's friendship.

I went at once to find Father and, of all places, tracked him down in the sewing room. He was wearing his dress

51

uniform and arguing with Baneet. "This uniform has shrunken, Baneet."

"No, Sahib James, you have grown fat as a mongoose."

"If you must let it out, do so, but I would rather not be compared to a mongoose."

I wished I didn't have to confront an irritated father, but I couldn't wait. "Father, I need to talk with you."

"I hope you haven't fallen into another bit of foolishness, Rosalind."

It was always a bad sign when father called me Rosalind instead of Rosy.

"No, something important has come up."

"You had better come into my study."

I hated his study, where I felt my years of scoldings scattered about the bookshelves and furniture to accuse me of past misdeeds. On the walls were photographs of the Indian troops that Father led in the war, and just below them a pair of prized Purdey rifles purchased long ago in England. Father didn't ask me to sit with him among the comfortable leather chairs, but placed himself behind his very large desk and left me standing like someone on trial. "Now what is it, Rosalind? I hope it's not trouble. I've had enough trouble for one day. There has been some question of whether the gold braid for the soldiers' turbans will be ready in time."

"It's about Aziz, Father."

"Who is Aziz?" Father seldom knew the names of the family members of his servants, and sometimes he forgot the servants' names, but surely he would know Amina.

"Aziz is Amina's son-in-law."

"If you are asking me to take on another servant, that is impossible. The wages I pay will destroy us."

"No, Aziz has no need for a job. He has a stall in the bazaar, and he sells very old ivory and jade."

"Nor is there any money for fake antiquities."

"They are not fake, they are beautiful." Why was it whenever I wanted to be at my best with Father, after two minutes of conversation we were arguing?

"There is no need to raise your voice, Rosalind. Come to the point."

"Aziz is in prison."

"That's what he gets for selling fake antiquities."

"You don't understand. He didn't sell anything fake."

"Are you suggesting the police arrest innocent people?"

"That is exactly what they have done, but it has nothing to do with selling. Aziz is a member of the Congress

53

Party, and the police are arresting the members, and that is why Aziz is in jail."

"The members of the Congress Party are responsible for the *hartal*. They hope their strike will send some sort of message to the Prince of Wales. If your Aziz is a member of that party, he deserves to be in jail. Now put all that nonsense out of your head. You should be thinking about parties and dresses. Your mother tells me Baneet is making you a lovely dress. I'm looking forward to showing off my pretty daughter at the receptions and parties."

When he began talking of parties and receptions, Father's voice lost its crossness. I knew now how I would free Aziz. "Yes, Father," I said with much meekness.

Immediately I went to my room, snatched up the money I had been given for clothes I never bought, the money with which I had tried to buy Nadi again, and hurried to the bazaar. With much bargaining I purchased raw cotton and a box *charkha*. I was going to learn to spin. I would make my own dress to show off to the prince, and I would let Father know what I was doing.

The next afternoon, when school was over, I found Sajala waiting for me. I told her, "First I will teach you, and then you will teach me." I showed an astonished Sajala my *charkha*.

We studied letters and division. Arithmetic was new to Sajala, and often she became discouraged and wanted to give up. "I am too stupid," she said, but she didn't run away.

Then it was Sajala's turn at instruction. She taught me how to make the *pooni*, a thin roll of cotton fiber from which I would draw out the yarn with my left hand while I turned the wheel of the *charkha* with my right hand. Over and over I tried to make my two hands do different things, and over and over the wheel went in the wrong direction and the yarn broke and had to be woven together. At one point, Sajala, who had hardly been brave enough to speak to me on our first day, was now laughing at me. She said, "You are very stupid." And I had to agree, but by the time the afternoon was over, I had a little spool of thread.

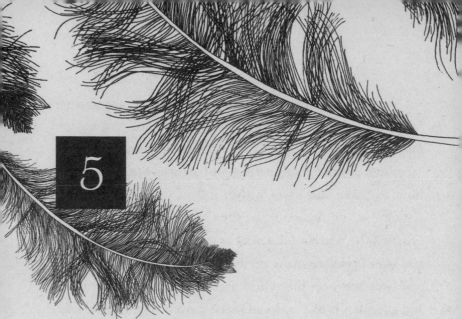

5

I carried my *charkha* everywhere. I sat with my *charkha*, one hand doing one thing and the other another. I took it with me to breakfast, lunch, and dinner. I had it in the late afternoons when we sat out on the veranda under the jacaranda trees sipping *nimbu pani*, squeezed from our own limes. I had the *charkha* after dinner when we opened the doors to the gardens to take in the fragrance of the Lady of the Night blossoms. At first everyone wanted to know what I was doing.

"Rosalind," Mother said, "whatever is that contraption?"

"It's a *charkha*," I said. "I'm learning how to spin."

"How very clever of you, Rosy," Aunt Louise said.

And from Aunt Ethyl, "Why in the world would you want to do that? It makes no sense."

Father said nothing. He knew all about Gandhi's scheme, but I guessed from his silence that he wouldn't give me the satisfaction of saying so.

It was an afternoon when we were all tired. Someone at the orphanage had come down with a rash, and my aunts had supervised a scrubbing of every inch of the orphanage, fearing a measles epidemic. At his office a subordinate had taken it upon himself to go against Father's orders. Mother had discovered that Baneet had made one of her dresses too short. At school, Bimal had put one of the many lizards he seemed always to have about him down Dev's *kurta*.

Talk lagged, and everyone was too tired and cross to do anything but watch me spin. Finally, Aunt Louise broke the silence. "What will you do with all that thread, Rosy, dear?"

"I'm going to have the weaver in the bazaar make it into a *khadi* dress for me to wear to the reception for the Prince of Wales. I think it's important for the prince to understand how the exporting of cotton to England and the importing of British cloth to India costs jobs for

Indians and makes clothing more expensive for them."

I had thrown a firecracker into the room. There was an explosion as everyone talked at once. Father was the loudest. "You are going to do no such thing. If you have any idea of appearing in a dress of that bizarre material, I personally will lock you in your room and turn the key."

Mother said, "Rosalind, dear, I went to all kinds of trouble to find just the right silk, and Baneet is making you the loveliest dress."

"Rosy," Aunt Louise murmured, "I do think you have gone just a bit too far. I am sure we all sympathize with your concerns, but we want to make things pleasant for the prince."

Aunt Ethyl was furious. "What can you be thinking, Rosalind? You would disgrace your father and bring shame on us all. I have never heard of so selfish an act. I sometimes think you cannot be British at all."

While the explosion continued, I sat quietly spinning until Father stalked off to his study, Mother went upstairs to her chaise longue, Aunt Ethyl followed Mother upstairs, making a point of slamming her bedroom door, and I was left with Aunt Louise.

"I'm doing it for Isha," I said, and I explained about

Aziz and how I wanted to goad Father into getting Aziz out of prison.

Aunt Louise shook her head. "It's not the way to go about it, Rosy. It's like prodding a donkey—the more you push, the more he digs in."

I wasn't sure Father would like being compared to a donkey, but I was beginning to think Aunt Louise right. "Then what can I do?"

"Your father must know exactly why you care so much what happens to Aziz. Let him see it is not about India's fight for freedom, though that may be a part of it, but because you care about Aziz and his family. You may not believe it, but your father has a heart as big as yours, though you have to dig a bit to reach it. And for heaven's sake, Rosy, do put that box thing away. The thread you have managed is appalling in its unevenness. Anything you weave from it would be too bumpy to wear. Now do go and have a talk with your father so we can live in peace again."

I didn't want to go back into the study with all those soldiers looking down from the wall, and the rifles, and the very large desk with Father sitting in majesty behind it. Still I went. I knocked faintly on the door, hoping he would not hear me.

"Yes?" It was an angry voice that answered me and an angry face that looked up at me.

"Father, Aziz's *suss*, Amina . . ."

He interrupted me, "For heaven's sake, speak English."

"Aziz's mother-in-law is Amina. She was my *ayah*, I mean my nurse, from the time I was born. You remember when the cobra crept close to my baby carriage and she beat it herself with a branch from a bauhinia tree. And then she took care of Mother all the while you were gone, and without Amina's coaxing and wheedling Mother might never have gotten up from her chaise longue. Isha, Amina's daughter, is my best friend. We grew up together and she taught me Hindi, and I know you don't like me to speak it, but just last week you told us you had promoted one of your assistants because he'd had the initiative to learn Hindi, and now Isha's husband, Aziz, is in prison, and Isha has the sweetest little boy, Eka, who can't stop smiling, and Isha is going to have another baby, and she is so unhappy about Aziz, which can't be good for her and for the baby that's coming, and if you will just get Aziz out of prison, I'll never touch a *charkha* again." I ran out of breath and awaited Father's anger.

"Rosy, I have always admired loyalty. It's a very British

quality. Now if you will excuse me, I have work to do."

He called me Rosy.

The next afternoon Isha, with Eka in her arms, came flying to the school. "Rosy, Aziz has come home! You are truly an angel of light, and your father is as well." Eka's smile was even brighter than usual. "Today I am all for the British," Isha said. "Even Aziz has a good word to say for the police who came into his cell with a *namaste* and treated him as a gentleman. Your father must have impressed the authorities. Should I go and fall at his feet?"

"That's the last thing he wants. Just keep Aziz out of trouble. I never want to go through something like that again. My thumb is sore from spinning, and all flattened out and ugly."

The minute I got home, I went in search of Father. I found him as usual in his study, but now the soldiers on the wall were grinning down at me. I made the dangerous journey past the desk to Father. I threw my arms around him. "Isha came and told me. She is so happy, and you should have seen Eka's smile."

"I'm sure I have no idea what you are talking about," he said, but he was grinning like Eka. "Whatever it is,"

Father said, "you are to make no mention of it to your Aunt Ethyl."

So for the first time, Father and I were on one side and Aunt Ethyl on the other.

I was pleased with myself and eager to tell Max what Father had done for Aziz. Max didn't have a lot of good things to say about British administrators like Father. He called them little tyrants. Maybe this would change his mind. I started off for the Nelsons' home, a large estate built with Mr. Nelson's jute profits, and entered through the formidable iron gates guarded by Chitt, a little *chota mali* who would not have kept anyone out, but then, the Nelsons are a welcoming family. Max was sitting in the garden with his mother and father. Mrs. Nelson was an imposing woman with square shoulders and muscled arms, probably from holding so many babies at her orphanage. She never bothered about her appearance but pulled her hair back in an untidy knot and must have worn whatever she first put her hand on in the morning.

Mr. Nelson, who owned the factory where the jute was cleaned, carded, and baled, had red hair and a reddish completion. He was large like Mrs. Nelson and had served in a cavalry unit in the war. Even in very hot weather he wore cavalry boots with spurs. "Well, Miss James," he said, "what devilment have you gotten into today?"

"Warner, let the girl be," Mrs. Nelson said. "Rosy, Safia came to the orphanage today with little Hari." She saw me wince to hear Nadi called that name. "Believe me, the child is well cared for. He was happy to see us, especially your Aunt Louise, who gave him so much love, but after the greetings and after we gave him treats and kisses, he turned to Safia and put up his arms."

"There, you see?" Max said. "All that fuss for nothing. Now let's escape from these ancient creatures."

The river was our favorite place. We hunkered down on the shore, sitting on a patch of grass that had sprung up during the summer monsoons. The fishermen were coming in after a day's work, the lucky ones with nets full of frantic fish slapping about. Tonight was the end of Diwali, the Indian holiday when little clay oil lamps are lit all over the city. Even the boats in the harbor had lamps, whose light was doubled in the water. Among the reeds, the fireflies added their own quick sparks.

I told Max all about Aziz and my weaving. He congratulated me on Aziz's release. "Well done, but did you know that Gandhi's followers went to him to complain that *khadi* cloth is too expensive for poor people to buy because it is all hand done? What do you think he told them? 'Wear fewer clothes,' he said, and immediately took off his *kameez* and hasn't put it back on. So as a follower of Gandhi you would be expected to do the same." Just when you think Max is being serious, there's a joke at the end of his lesson.

"I'm finished with spinning, and I'm not wearing *khadi* to the ball. I'm to have a frock of blue silk."

"Rosy, I write for a political journal, not a fashion journal."

"And I'm to dazzle the prince. I may even dance with him."

Max looked at me in a strange way. I thought he might be angry with me for going on about the prince. "I'm only teasing," I said.

"You've given me an idea. Of course I would have to get the permission of the Congress Party, but I'm sure they would go along. I might get an article out of it for *Young India*."

Max had already been questioned by the police for an article he had written about how few Indians there were in the Civil Service. Instead it was the British who were the civil servants administrating the country. The article had come to the attention of my father, who had been Max's commanding officer during the war. Father stormed about after reading the article. "It's that outrageous lieutenant of mine," Father said. "I'll have his hide." But cooler heads kept Max safe.

I asked Max why the authorities didn't close down *Young India*.

Max said, "The British powers that be are content to channel all the criticism against them into one magazine they can keep an eye on. They think if the Indian people have somewhere to complain, they will be satisfied. Of course they are too blind to see that the Indian people have had enough. The very fact that they are talking about closing shops and schools all through India when the Prince comes should open the eyes of the British. It isn't just Gandhi, it's hundreds of thousands who want Britain out of India."

I was suspicious. "What is this article you're planning, and what does it have to do with me?"

"We've been trying to discover how we can get our message to the prince while he's here in Calcutta. They're keeping any dissenters a million miles away, but some of

Gandhi's people believe if the prince knew how much the Indian people long for freedom, he would take that message back to his father, the king. Gandhi has written a letter to the king explaining all that. Now all we need is someone who can get past the prince's guards and past the police and give the prince the letter."

When I saw the expression on Max's face as he looked at me, my heart dropped. "What are you thinking?"

But he wouldn't tell me.

After Max left, I thought more about the visit of the prince. I began to see that with my excitement over my clothes and the parties and the possibility of actually seeing the prince, I was no different from Amy and Sarah. I thought of what the visit meant to the Indian people and how Aziz had been imprisoned. Hundreds of Indians had been imprisoned as he had, and they did not have an influential man like Father to come to their aid. I would go to Calcutta, but I would not go as a silly girl who cared only about seeing the Prince of Wales.

6

It was my day for visiting Nadi. In spite of Safia's unhappy looks, I still called him Nadi, but each visit showed me how he was becoming more Hari and less Nadi. He was chattering more, but always in Hindi. When I spoke English, he no longer understood me.

I found Safia washing clothes at the mangrove swamp where I had first seen her. When I saw Nadi splashing about with his brothers and the other children, his little arms and legs covered with mud, I hardly recognized him. Yet clearly he was happy. The others included him in their game of frog catching, and when he slipped in the mud, they cheerfully put him back on his feet.

"Safia, I have a favor to ask."

At once she was on the defensive. "You don't take my Hari."

"No, nothing like that. I can see he's happy with you, it's only that I want him to be able to be a part of my world, too. I can speak Hindi, but my aunts can't, and they would love to watch him grow up, and one day he will want to go to school or find a job, and English will help him. In the Indian Civil Service they speak English, and to do many businesses you must have English."

Safia looked puzzled. The words "school" and "Civil Service" had nothing to do with her life or with Iravat's and they did not "find" a job. They inherited jobs as sweepers or whatever was allowed untouchables.

"Nadi doesn't have to have the same life you and Iravat have." When I saw her expression, I said, "I don't mean there is anything wrong with your life. No, I do mean that. You shouldn't have to be limited to what other people say you can do. You should be free to be what you want."

At the word "free" she looked about as if it were a dangerous word, and indeed for her it was. Quickly, I said, "I only want to see him a couple of times a week to teach him English before he forgets what he knows of the language.

That way, we can all talk with him and understand what he is thinking and he will know what we are thinking."

She shrugged. "I don't care. Just so you don't take him away to do your teaching. I have to have my eyes on him. Also, please, his name is Hari, not Nadi."

After that, I called him only Hari, but it was a long time before I could think of him as anyone but Nadi. Now that I had Safia's permission, I called Nadi to me. "Hari," I said, "let me give you some words." He grinned at me. I held his strong little arms that might have been twisted and limp but for Isha's warning, Mrs. Nelson's orphanage, and my buying him from Pandy.

"Mud," I said, rubbing the muck away.

"Mud," he repeated.

I took his hand and walked with him to the river. "Water." I pointed to an osprey in its nest high in a banyan tree. "Bird," I said, and Nadi repeated the word, smiling as if I were giving him something and he was receiving it.

Safia never took her eyes from us. She wasn't ready to trust me, but when Nadi was quick to repeat a word, she smiled with pride.

After that, I came several times a week. Sometimes I brought him a little gift, but I had to be careful. If the gift was something of value, Safia was worried that I was trying to lure him away. If it was a pretty flower or a shell I had found along the shore, Safia was happy, for those were things she might give as well. Nadi was as pleased with a shell as he would have been with a costly toy, for he was interested in everything.

The newspapers were full of the coming visit of the Prince of Wales. In my little school I was kept busy answering questions. The visit was spoken of everywhere, and the boys in my class were curious. They wanted to know all about the prince. I told them, "He lives with his parents, the king and queen, in an enormous house with hundreds of rooms. His great-grandmother was Queen Victoria." These boys, like all Indian children who attended the schools set up for them by the British government, knew Queen Victoria, for her picture was sure to be on the wall of every classroom.

"His granny is very fat," Dev said. "She must eat a lot of *kheer*."

Manu asked, "Why is there a *hartal* before the royal prince comes?"

Bimal said, "He will come, and there will be no store

open for him if he wants a *topee* to put on his head."

I tried to explain. "The *hartal* isn't because the Prince of Wales is a bad man. Gandhi has called for the *hartal* because he wants the prince to know how much the Indian people long for freedom from the prince's country." I often talked with the boys about the British rule of India and how Indians were not allowed to make decisions for themselves but had to do what the British government said. I explained to them why they were no longer going to the school the British had set up for Indian children. They sat quietly listening to my explanation of the *hartal*, and when I finished, I was sure they understood, for there was no more asking about the prince and his great-granny, but something in their silence was troubling. The silence was directed toward me, while between themselves they exchanged quick glances and private smiles. It was the next afternoon, when I arrived at school to find the classroom empty, that I understood.

On the blackboard, written in bold letters, was a single word: HARTAL. It was like a slap in the face. Did my teachings lead them to see me as the enemy? Had I taught them to dislike me because I was British? Had all my good work gone for nothing?

Sajala came as usual, moving gracefully as a butterfly out of the shrubbery in her *salwar kameez*. "Sajala, where are your brother and the other boys? What do they mean, *hartal*? Why should they strike against me? I'm their friend."

"I only came to tell you I'm sorry that I can't do my lesson with you. Dev says British schools must be closed, and he says I must not come anymore."

"But this isn't a British school. It's just me. The government has nothing to do with it like they do with the school the boys went to. That school was shut down by Gandhi because it was run by the British government."

"Dev and the other boys say, "Rosalind *Memsahib* is our dear friend, but we want to tell the prince India must have freedom. We want our own *hartal*.""

"But, Sajala, their foolishness shouldn't affect you. You are doing so well with your lessons. How will Dev know if you come?"

Out of the corner of her eye, Sajala looked pointedly at some nearby plumbago shrubs. "Dev," I called, "come out and talk with me."

After a minute's wait, Dev ventured out, gray stains on his arms from the sap of the plumbago branches. He kept his distance. "Dev, you must tell the boys to come back. I have permission from the strike committee to have the school. They don't want you to lose time while the British schools are closed. They know that I am on India's side. So it's all right for me to teach you."

"You have a British mother. You have a British father. I see him each morning on the way to the Civil Service, where they make up their rules for us."

"I don't agree with my father. I do and say what I want to."

Sajala let out a little gasp. Dev looked shocked. He said, "It is shameful that you disobey your father. Sajala and I would never do such a thing."

"But you just criticized me for having a father who worked for the Civil Service. Now you criticize me because I don't agree with him."

"He is your father. You must do as he says."

"But surely I don't have to say what he says."

Dev said, "How can we be taught by someone who is disrespectful? The lessons would be bad lessons."

"You don't understand, Dev. I do respect my father, but I have my own ideas."

"Would you throw those ideas in your father's face?"

"Of course not, but that doesn't mean I shouldn't do what I think is right."

"And will there be a scolding if you do?"

Reluctantly, I had to admit that I was often scolded. The image of me being roundly chastised by my father for my sins seemed to satisfy Sajala and Dev, and so I went on, "Dev, we won't have the school, but please let me talk with the boys." Dev liked to be in charge of things. I was sure he had been the one to inspire the *hartal*. Knowing that, I said, "I don't suppose the boys would come just because you asked them."

Dev looked offended. "If I tell them to come, they will come."

"Then please tell them. And though there will be no school, tell them to bring their notebooks."

Goral arrived first, then Manu, who shyly gave me a hibiscus blossom, looking about to be sure Dev was not there to see him. Ishat came with Dev and with Bimal, who with more time on his hands had found more lizards.

"I will respect your *hartal*," I said. Dev looked at the other boys to be sure they were sufficiently aware of his triumph. "But I miss all of you. I must see you every day or I will be unhappy."

Manu moved closer to Bimal and me and gave me one of his smaller lizards to enjoy. The shy lizard disappeared into my sleeve. "We won't have a school," I said. "We won't go inside. Instead we will sit here under the bo trees and play games."

The boys thought that a great idea. Goral said, "We could play Chaupar. I'll get my board and some cowrie shells."

Chaupar had been played in India for five hundred years. It was played on boards marked in squares. I played it with Max, who delighted in telling me that instead of cowrie shells, the Emperor of Akbar used sixteen girls from his harem as pawns. The game was addictive, and I had no intention of spending my afternoons playing Chaupar with my students.

"The first game we will play is a spelling game. We will see who will be first to get all the English words correct." I then went through the list they had for their homework. They were disappointed. They would have preferred Chaupar, but after a bit they fought to see who would be first. In the same way we went on to do our fractions.

Not for one minute were the boys fooled, but they had their *hartal*, and I had my classes. We were all happy. Since we were under the bo trees and not in a classroom, no one complained of Sajala sitting quietly nearby listening to every word.

Later, when I told Max how I had managed, he laughed and patted me on the head. "Rosy, that's brilliant. What an excellent politician you would make." Nothing pleased me more than Max's praise.

7

The club held its annual costume ball each year
on the last Saturday in October. Everyone went, and everyone wore a costume. Father fussed and fumed as he did
every year, but if you didn't dress up, you were considered
a poor sport. Finally, he succumbed to Mother's pleading.
He decided to go as Lord Nelson, the great British naval
hero who won lots of battles and died very bravely at the
Battle of Trafalgar. Father wore a three-cornered hat and,
on his uniform, lots of gold braid and dangling metals.
Nelson had lost his right arm during a battle, and Father
practiced keeping his arm inside his uniform, letting the
empty sleeve dangle in a very scary way.

Nelson was rather a naughty man, and even though he was married, he was madly in love with Emma, Lady Hamilton, who was gorgeous. She was also daring, and it was said that she once danced naked on a dining room table. Naturally, Mother was going as Emma, but a fully clothed Lady Hamilton with a flowing gown and a marvelous hat with yards of ribbon and veiling.

I couldn't imagine what Aunt Ethyl would wear, but I shouldn't have been surprised. She was planning to go as Britannia, the figure representing British power. Britannia is always shown as this giant lady warrior with a helmet, a trident, and a shield. Father found for her a German helmet he had brought back from the war as a souvenir. Aunt Ethyl fashioned a shield from cardboard. The trident, which is a sort of fishing spear, Ranjit borrowed for her from his cousin who is a fisherman.

When I asked Aunt Louise how she would dress, she confessed, "I've always longed to wear a *sari*. This would be a perfect time." Aunt Ethyl was shocked, but Father said, "Half the club will be dressed as Indians. We'll have plenty of women in *saris*, and men as Indian Sikhs with turbans and Indian princes in robes." I thought this very ironic since Indians were absolutely forbidden in the club except as servants.

I took Aunt Louise to the bazaar to shop for a suitable *sari*. She loved the bazaar, but she was so much under Aunt Ethyl's eye, she seldom got there. Once there, however, you couldn't get her away. She admired the brightly colored kites in every shape and size. She lingered over a pair of earrings at the bangle shop, holding them up to her ears and laughing at the reflection in the stall's cracked mirror. There were seductive things to eat—spun sugar that got all over your face, and sherbet in flavors such as mango and melon. There was the coconut man who slashed off the top of a coconut with one sweep of his scimitar and gave the coconut to you so you could drink its sweet milk.

Aunt Louise avoided the ear-cleaning man and kept her distance from the man piping away to a cobra that inched its way out of a basket, swaying in a giddy way. The most generous person in the world, someone who gave almost all she had to the poor, Aunt Louise would not give an *anna* to the pitiful child beggars who had purposely been crippled. "The money doesn't go to the poor children, but to evil men like that Pandy person who would have twisted Nadi's little limbs."

At the *sari* shop she picked up one *sari* and then another. "I must have this pale lavender that is just the color of the jacaranda blossoms, or this yellow *sari* the color of the mustard fields. Oh, Rosy, I can't make up my mind." At last she chose a *sari* the pale coral color of the inside of a seashell. When she had made her purchase, I coaxed her back to the bangle shop for the earrings she had admired.

The minute we got home, she sent for Amina to teach her how to wind the six meters of cloth into a dress. Their giggles could be heard all over the house, causing a disapproving Aunt Ethyl to paint with defiant brushstrokes a British flag on her shield so there would be no question of *her* sympathies.

For myself, I had decided to be an Odissi dancer, a classical dancer who danced to honor Lord Krishna, one of the Indian deities. I convinced Baneet to make me a divided skirt. I borrowed Isha's bangles for my arms and made bracelets of bells for my ankles and a kind of jeweled crown.

I was pleased with my costume and wandered over in the afternoon to the Nelsons' to brag about it to Max. I found Max and his friend, Raman Mehra, lounging about in the Nelsons' garden. I loved the garden, with its strutting peacocks, its rosebushes, and its trellises covered with crimson and pink bougainvilleas, and Mrs. Nelson's favorite jasmine shrubs sent up a heady fragrance.

I had met Raman before at the Nelsons' home. The Nelsons were one of only a few British families in whose homes Indians were welcome. Raman had been at Cambridge with Max, and before Cambridge, Raman's wealthy family had sent him to Eton, England's most prestigious boarding school. There were only one or two Englishmen in our town who could boast of having attended Eton. Raman's father was a well-known solicitor who was often in the British courts trying to extract members of the Congress Party from prison. Raman's father wanted him to return to England to study the law so he could join his father's firm, but Raman didn't want to leave India. He insisted, "I can do more good working with Max on *Young India.*" The magazine was read by all the supporters of Gandhi and had infuriated the British by printing Gandhi's call for a *hartal* all over the country on the day of the arrival in India of the Prince of Wales.

In his call for the *hartal* Gandhi had said, "His Royal Highness will soon be in our midst. I should advise a boycott of all public functions held in his honor. He is a personable and amenable English gentleman, but in my humble opinion, public interest demands that this official visit should be strictly ignored. His Royal Highness comes to sustain a corrupt system of government, he comes to whitewash an irresponsible bureaucracy, he comes to make us forget the unforgettable."

I thought it the most inspiring thing I had ever read, but when Father heard about it, he gnashed his teeth and vowed to burn every copy of *Young India* he could get his hands on.

Max greeted me from his reclining chair, but Raman had beautiful manners and got up at once when he saw me to offer me his own chair and pour me some tea. I was always flustered when I was near him. He was so elegant and so handsome, with his dark eyes and white teeth and soft words and very mischievous grin.

Max said, "Rosy, tell us something to amuse us."

I described my dancing-girl costume, not bothering to ask about Max's costume, for he never went to the club if he could help it. So I was surprised when he said, "I'm going as Caesar. Mother is giving me an old sheet for a toga, and I'll make a laurel wreath from neem leaves. What do you think of that? What's more, I'm bringing a friend."

"It will be much more fun with you there. Who's your friend?"

"He was with me at Cambridge, the smartest fellow there."

"Oh, I don't know about that," Raman said.

"What is he doing in India?"

"Actually, he lives right here in this town."

I went over the names of the young men who had been at Cambridge with Max. There were only two I could think of. "It can't be Jonathan Marks or Tommy Writhin." I was sure he wouldn't spend time with either of them. Max considered both Jonathon and Tommy "sticks," typically British with no love of India, staying on in this country for what they could get out of it. The only reason they tolerated Max and his advanced ideas was that Max's father was one of the richest men in our town. Besides, Jonathan was working for the Civil Service in Bombay, and Tommy was in the infirmary after breaking his leg while playing polo.

Max shook his head. "No, not Jonathan or Tommy. Someone you will probably find most attractive."

Raman said, "Max, stop teasing Rosalind." There was a mysterious smile on his face. "Shall we let her in on our secret? She might be helpful."

"Can we trust you, Rosy?"

"You know you can. Tell!"

"Raman is going with me."

For once I didn't know what to say. Raman was hardly a servant, so how could he be at the club when Indians were strictly forbidden? I felt my face turn red, and I stared intently at an enormous ant carrying a bit of leaf.

"I know what you are thinking, Rosy. Raman is going to be booted out, right?"

Raman said, "Don't lead her on, Max."

"You've got to swear you won't say a word. Raman and I have a scheme. You know how all the members at the club love to dress up as Indians. Well, I'm going to pass Raman off as Ashton Jeffers, an old, very British Cambridge friend here on a visit. Just think how furious everyone would be if they knew."

"What about your parents?"

"Dad's away at one of the jute plantations, and Mother isn't keen on costume balls."

At first the idea terrified me, but the more I thought about it, the more intrigued I became. Why couldn't Raman bring it off? After all those years in England, Raman's speech was certainly that of a well-educated Englishman. His complexion was darker, but all the imitation Indians at the club would be wearing makeup. "And what will you go as?" I asked.

"I will go as I am!" Though Raman laughed, I thought I saw a flicker of doubt cross his face.

The night of the ball, the club was festive, drowning in flowers inside and out. Tiny lights like fireflies were strung on the trees in the garden. White-uniformed Indian servants glided silently about filling glasses and passing dishes of boring British food. People exclaimed over everyone's costumes, laughing and teasing. Mother was gorgeous and a great success as Lady Hamilton. At the last moment my aunts had second thoughts and had to be coaxed into attending, but when they began to mix with all the kings and queens and Indian princes and characters from Shakespeare, they felt right at home.

Amy, who was dressed as Alice in Wonderland, her long yellow hair held back with a band and an apron tied around her schoolgirl's dress, looked enviously at my costume. "Rosalind, you are too glamorous." A moment later, Robin Meath, a regular at the club, swept me away to the dance floor. The orchestra was playing the sentimental, "I'll Be With You in Apple Blossom Time," and I was squeezed in Robin's pythonlike embrace and trying to breathe when Max walked in with Raman.

"Why have you stopped dancing?" Robin said.

"I'm sorry. It's a little warm in here. I think I need some air." I made my escape. A minute later I joined Max and Raman, who were chatting with the club president, Malcolm MacGregor. "You say you were at Eton, my boy. Ashton Jeffers? I do believe that name is familiar. Of course, that was long after my time, but I dare say it's not much changed. I suppose you had your share of birching and boiled potatoes. Well, I can't tell you what a pleasure this is. You must dine with Mrs. MacGregor and myself. Now go and have a dance with the lovely Rosalind here."

Raman paused for a moment and then took me in his arms. He was a graceful dancer. "Where did you learn to dance so well?" I asked.

"Max gave me instructions. You would have enjoyed seeing the two of us waltzing around. Rosalind, I'm beginning to be sorry I'm doing this. That man was very nice."

"He wouldn't have been nice if he knew you were an Indian."

"It's been very confusing coming back to India from England. At Cambridge they were used to foreign students. They accepted me for what I was. Here, with my British accent, I feel alienated, I've forgotten how to be an

Indian. The other Indians on the magazine are suspicious of me. They don't really think I'm against the British rule. They think I'm a British spy."

The musicians had paused, and as Raman and I were talking I saw Max coming toward us with my father in tow. I was unhappy. I didn't want Father to be a part of this game. I could imagine how furious he would be should he ever find out.

Max said, "Rosy, your father wanted to be introduced to my friend, Ashton Jeffers, from Cambridge. I explained that Jeffers was visiting for a few days and I had brought him along tonight promising him pretty girls, and you see he has found one."

Father shook hands with Raman. "You make a very convincing Indian prince," he said, "and I'm sure Rosy has enjoyed meeting you. Max hasn't said what you are doing in India, Jeffers. Are you thinking of joining the British Civil Service? We can always use fine students like you. Max has told me you took a first at Cambridge."

"If Max has been putting about my virtues, I'm afraid he has made me into something of an imposter, sir. As to the British Civil Service, I'm afraid they wouldn't have me. The truth is, I can't quite find a place for myself in India."

At least Raman had spoken nothing but the truth to Father, even if Father didn't know what that truth was.

"Well," Father said, "India does take a bit of getting used to. The Indian people are not like you and me, Jeffers, but I'd be glad to put in a word for you with the Civil Service. Just let Max here know. I am sure you are an excellent example for Max, an example he badly needs." Father turned to Max. "I must say, young man, that lately I've had no reports of any mischief you have been up to. I hope this means you have finally gotten some sense. Now if you young people will excuse me, I'll let you enjoy yourselves."

Max could hardly contain his laughter until Father was out of earshot. "The British Civil Service. What a hoot. Wouldn't I love to see his face if he knew. It would be almost worth taking the blame."

Raman's voice lost all of its warmth and friendliness. "Don't be a fool, Max. I had no business being a part of this game. Now I'm leaving."

Raman strode past the Indian servants, who looked at him and then quickly away. They hadn't been fooled. A minute later I felt a tight grasp. Aunt Louise was holding on to Max with her other arm. "I want to see the two of you outside." I was surprised at her strength as she pulled us into an unoccupied part of the garden. Gone was the pleasure and excitement she had shown over wearing her *sari*. Instead I saw an expression that was clearly anger.

"Max, have you forgotten that I met Raman at your house when I was visiting your mother?"

"Aunt Louise, you won't give us away?"

"Rosalind, I want you and Max to explain to me what Raman was doing here posing as an Ashton Jeffers?"

I cringed. It was the first time Aunt Louise had ever called me Rosalind. It was like a slap.

"It was all my fault, Miss Hartley. Rosy had nothing to do with it. It was just a joke."

"And a very bad one. Just because the people here tonight are foolish enough to believe they are better than the countrymen among whom they live and whom they profit by and whom they oppress, that is no reason to encourage Raman to lower himself by participating in this charade. What of Raman's dignity? I am disappointed in both of you." With that, Aunt Louise left us.

"I don't see what it's got to do with her," Max said. But Max had flushed a bright red. He understood very well what we had done, and all our pleasure in the evening was at an end. We sat next to the pool, all the dancing and chattering going on around us, too ashamed to say a word to each other.

I had a troubled night. Next morning at breakfast, Father said, "That young Jeffers fellow who was a friend of Max's from Cambridge seems a very polite sort. Max could take a lesson from him."

I couldn't help looking across the table at Aunt Louise, who had the faintest smile on her lips, and I knew I was forgiven.

8

On November 17 His Majesty's ship, the *Renown*, steamed into Bombay harbor with flags flying, and the Prince of Wales stepped for the first time on Indian soil. Those supporting Gandhi's *hartal* stayed away, and their homes and businesses were hung with black bunting, but thousands of loyalists, both British and Indian, lined the streets and the rooftops to cheer the prince.

We all devoured the description of the prince's arrival in the *Times of India*. It described the sun climbing a cloudless sky and the roar of a salute fired by the guns of the East Indian Squadron. The prince was greeted by Lord Reading, the man the British had chosen to rule over India. Lord Reading was impressive in a white pith *topee* and a gray morning coat with the Star of India pinned on it. Present were all the *maharajas* in "shimmering silks and jeweled *pagaris*." In return for their loyalty and a lot of money, the British allowed these Indian princes to rule over their enormously wealthy kingdoms set within India like so many emeralds and rubies set into a crown.

The parade went on through the city of Bombay for five miles. Father was delighted to read that in addition to whole regiments of British artillery and cavalry, there were Indian Muslim solders like his Gurkhas wearing uniforms of scarlet and gold, their leaders carrying golden fans and purple umbrellas embroidered in gold. Father would lead his own battalion of Gurkhas when the prince came to Calcutta.

The newspaper also said that in another part of Bombay, Gandhi had been up at seven in the morning to make a fiery speech and to call for a bonfire of foreign cloth. Those who had come to greet the prince tangled with those returning from Gandhi's speech, and there were terrible riots. Several people were killed and many wounded. The prisons were filled, and Gandhi was so upset at the fighting he began a fast, refusing food until the violence on both sides stopped.

Father fumed at the article about the demonstrations. "They want their necks wrung!" He looked like he would love to run into the streets and wring the first necks he could get his hands on.

Aunt Ethyl said, "What can the poor king and queen think of this country's welcome for their son?"

Mother took to her chaise longue and consumed glasses of chilled *nimbu pani*, while Aunt Louise said, "I am sure the dear boy will understand how such things can happen because of the Indian people's longing for freedom." But she said it when Father and Aunt Ethyl were out of the room.

Day by day we followed the prince's journey up and down India, Max with great amusement and scorn. Max, Raman, and I were sitting on the Nelsons' veranda having tea and nibbling on macaroons imported from England. As Max turned the pages of the newspaper he said to me, "Your prince is spending his time going on hunts, leaving a trail of dead animals all over the country."

I had to admit it was true. While the prince made ceremonial speeches and attended receptions, there were also reports of hunting parties of the most exotic kind. The *maharaja* of Kolhapur lent the prince's party his cheetah. This amazing animal was let loose to kill deer! In another place there was a fight staged between a wild boar and a trained leopard, with the leopard finally killing the boar. A couple of days later the prince's party was after gazelles, and a few days after that, crocodiles. Even birds didn't escape. On December third it was recorded that the prince shot thirty-five grouse.

I announced, "The *Times* says His Highness was the guest of the *maharaja* of Bharatpur yesterday."

With great scorn Max said, "Yes, your prince chased bucks at fifty miles an hour in the *maharaja*'s Rolls-Royce. Quite the sportsman."

"He's not *my* prince." That was not entirely true. I had been eagerly reading every detail about the prince I could get my hands on, but now, looking through Max's eyes, I could see my idol had faults.

Raman said, "I am sure Rosalind would not want to claim ownership of such a man."

I had been afraid that after the masquerade party Raman would never want to see me again, but unlike Max, Raman was easier going, he cared deeply about freedom for his country, but he still had friends like Max and me. I think that's why he had felt so bad about deceiving Father.

"The prince," said Max, "goes about India in a train with a separate car to hold twenty polo ponies lent him by the *maharajas*."

Raman said, "At least when he's playing polo he's not killing some defenseless creature."

"You're only excusing him, Raman, because you like polo yourself."

"And why shouldn't I like polo? Polo has been played in India since the thirteenth century, though unfortunately the British have taken over our game."

That was true, for every day, you could see on the *maidan* men on their ponies, which weren't little ponies at all but specially trained horses. They knocked about balls with mallets, viciously cutting in front of one another to get the ball into their side's goal. There was always chatter of polo matches, which were divided into *chukkers*, and there was much talk of who had the best pony and who had gotten the most goals and who had broken their legs or arms, which happened quite often. Of course Indians weren't allowed on the polo teams, but I had heard from

Max that Raman had played polo at Cambridge and was an excellent player. He often went very early in the mornings to the *maidan*, where there were one or two British players who so admired Raman's skill that he was invited to play informally with them and actually give them pointers.

"Can I watch you some morning, Raman?"

"Of course, but there won't be much to see. I'm nothing special."

Max was indignant. "You are a hundred times better than those fools at the club who bounce around on their ponies. I don't know why you lower yourself to sneak out to the *maidan* when the regular teams won't have you."

"I'm not sneaking. I'm up there on top of a horse for everyone to see. It's either that or I don't play at all, and I like to play. How else would I get a horse if they didn't lend one to me? With you, Max, it's all or nothing. Life isn't like that. I'm not going to put everything on hold while I wait for freedom to come to my country. I want to live a little. I don't see anything wrong in that."

"While you're on your polo pony, your fellow Indians are risking their lives."

"I don't see you risking your life. Writing for a magazine is all we do. Where is the danger in that? Where is the sacrifice in your coming home each night to a luxurious home like this and Indian servants to pick up your socks and underpants and serve you tea and imported macaroons that cost as much as a servant would make in a month?"

I was sure they would come to blows. I knew that Max did truly care for India's freedom, however much he hid it behind the jokes he made. "Stop it!" I ordered. "If you start fighting between yourselves, we'll never get anyplace."

Max had the grace to be shamefaced. "All right. I give in. You can have your stupid ponies if I can have my macaroons. The question is what we can do when the prince comes to Calcutta. We don't have anyone who can get close to the prince to give him our message. Gandhi wrote an appeal for India's freedom in *Young India* that would move any person with sense."

Raman said, "The prince's handlers keep from him anyone who might tell the truth. He's surrounded every minute. He'll never get to see the real India."

"What if we knew someone who would be sipping tea with His Royal Highness at garden parties in Calcutta and dancing with him at balls?"

At once I knew whom Max meant. "Don't look at

me, Max. I'm going to be just one of hundreds of people at those parties. I'll never get to actually meet the prince."

"Why couldn't you faint in his arms or do whatever girls do to get some poor fellow's attention?"

Raman said, "You have no business involving Rosalind in your mad scheme."

Max sighed and turned back to the newspaper. "I see they went tiger hunting today in Bhikna Thori. The prince and the other brave men all climbed up on elephants, made a circle around some poor tiger, and shot it. What good sport!"

"That's disgusting." Tigers were gorgeous creatures. "Go ahead and give me your message to give to him. I can always dress up like a tiger or a crocodile to get his attention."

"That's my girl," Max said. He gave me a look of approval, and Max's acceptance meant much to me.

Raman shot him a disgusted look. "Rosalind shouldn't be involved in your dirty work."

"Since when is working for the freedom of India, which is your country, dirty work?"

"I don't recall asking you to work for the freedom of my country. I believe it was your idea. The Indians are perfectly capable of gaining their own freedom without the help of an Englishman."

It was time for my tutoring session, and I left them to their arguments, not for a minute taking Max's suggestion or my agreement seriously. I didn't believe I would be close to the prince, and if I were, I would be too terrified to do more than curtsy. Certainly I wouldn't sidle up to the Prince of Wales and slip into his pocket an incendiary message from someone who would like nothing better than to see him out of India.

I found an excited Mr. Snartwell. His wife was with him, and they both looked like children who had been given a treat. "Miss James," Mr. Snartwell announced, "the most extraordinary thing has happened. I have been invited to Calcutta to assist the Bengal governor, the Earl of Ronaldshay, in writing his speech of welcome for the prince."

I wasn't surprised. After all, in England, Mr. Snartwell was known as a great scholar of English literature. "Congratulations, I am so pleased for you."

"Of course I won't actually be writing the speech, just adding a few decorations, a little frill here and there to make the speech go down well. They'll want a bit of

Shakespeare, of course, and a line or two of Milton and something from the King James Bible. Even a touch of Kipling wouldn't go amiss." He recited:

> The poor little street-bred people that vapour
> and fume and brag,
> They are lifting their heads in the stillness to
> yelp at the English Flag!

"Oh, no!" I said. "I don't think that's a good idea. Gandhi's followers will think you are talking about them."

"Ah, but that isn't what Kipling meant at all. The 'poor little street-bred people' are the English themselves, who don't appreciate the county they have conquered, India, but perhaps you are right. There is also this Kipling, but I'm afraid I would never get away with it:

> But there is neither East nor West, Border, nor
> Breed, nor Birth,
> When two strong men stand face to face, tho'
> they come from the ends of the earth!

"Oh, please try," I said, and thought of Raman atop his

horse, every bit as good as the British polo players.

Mrs. Snartwell brought in tea. I was surprised to see that for the first time there were biscuits to go with it. "I thought we might have just a bit of a celebration," Mrs. Snartwell said.

"My wife has been invited to accompany me."

"I am not sure I can go," she said.

"Nonsense, Wilfreda, of course you must come with me."

I remembered how excited she was when I told her our family was invited. "Why ever wouldn't you, Mrs. Snartwell?"

"Jeffery, I wonder if I might just steal Miss James for a moment. I need her advice."

"Yes, of course, my dear, but don't keep her too long. We are reviewing our hendecasyllables today."

I was gently led to Mrs. Snartwell's closet. It was opened, and inside were a half dozen of the same brownish, grayish objects that were more like withered leaves than dresses. "You see, my dear, I have nothing to wear, and I can't ask Jeffery for money; he doesn't have it. The trip and our accommodations will be paid for by the governor, but he will send no money for a dress. You understand what clothes are needed on such occasions. I couldn't go in one of these and shame Jeffery, but I daren't tell him why."

At once I knew the solution. "Plan on going and leave the rest to me." I left a puzzled Mrs. Snartwell and returned to Mr. Snartwell and the dreaded hendecasyllables.

The next day, I arrived at the Snartwells with a package that I handed to Mrs. Snartwell, first drawing her aside so Mr. Snartwell did not hear me. "Mother hopes you won't mind, but she wants you to have these. She has dozens, and we all want you to go to Calcutta more than anything." In the package were a garden-party dress and a ball gown.

She wasn't at all embarrassed, but grabbed the package out of my hands, giving me some idea of the strength of her dreams and the sentence of hard labor she had been under all those years.

Mr. Snartwell and I were having a cozy talk about the resemblance of Old English verse to Germanic war poems when Mrs. Snartwell entered the room in a swirl of chiffon. In trying on the dress her red curls had loosened. They fell about her face, which was flushed a becoming pink. The ugly oxfords had been discarded, and barefoot, she was an enchanting wood nymph.

"Wilfreda!" Mr. Snartwell, probably for the first time in his life, was wordless, but not for long. "There is no need, my dear, for my little poetic ornaments and tricks. You will provide all the witchery needed."

With that, we returned to the Germanic war poems.

9

I went early one morning to watch Raman play polo. I didn't tell Max, not wanting him there to make fun of Raman for playing a game Max despised. I took a rickshaw to the *maidan*. There were all the signs of an Indian morning. Along the riverbank, people were chattering back and forth to one another while they brushed their teeth and had their baths. Pye-dogs barked and snarled, digging amid the rubbish for the few scraps of food. Brahmin cows, one with a garland of marigold around her neck, wandered in the streets, making the rickshaws and *tongas* dart around them with a frantic ringing of bells. Families who had slept on the street rolled up their blankets and wandered off. For a long moment I thought of what the day would be for them, but the morning was bright and cool, and I was going to see Raman and, later in the day, try on my new ball gown. I forgot the homeless families as if in my not thinking of them, their troubles would disappear.

It wasn't a regular game. Raman and Martin Banister were mounted on ponies whose legs and tails were bound up so nothing would get in the way of their speed. I had seen Martin at the club. His father was very rich from exporting cotton to England. As far as I knew, Martin didn't do much of anything but play polo. The two men were knocking a ball about, riding at each other and slinging their mallets in a ferocious way, making circles and figure eights, turning this way and that. After a few minutes, they stopped and a servant brought in new ponies, and Raman and Martin started up all over again.

I watched Martin ride right at Raman, cutting him off and nearly making him fall from his horse. "Foul!" Raman called out. "What's the matter with you, Banister? You crossed the line of the ball."

Raman and his pony seemed to be a single thing. Even I could see how often he bettered Martin, knocking the ball through the goalposts.

Finally, Martin threw his mallet down in disgust. "That's enough for me! There must be something wrong with my ponies today. You can replace the divots, Raman."

The hooves of the ponies had dug up divots of earth, leaving big dimples in the grass. "That's a job for both of us, Banister," Raman said, but Martin just stalked away. Raman shrugged, and I winced as I watched him obediently do what Martin had ordered. I was glad Max wasn't there to see.

Raman spotted me and, after he had replaced the clumps of grass, walked over to me. "Well, what do you think of polo?"

"You ride so well, but I thought you would both get killed. Those mallets are deadly, and you swing them around as if they were no more than flyswatters. Why did the two of you change horses?"

"All the hard riding and twisting about is very hard on the horses. In a regular game everyone changes horses at the end of a *chukker*—that's every six minutes—and there are at least four *chukker* in a game."

"But it would cost a fortune to have that many ponies."

"Remember the twenty polo ponies the prince travels with? It's why polo is called the Game of Kings. By the time you pay for all your ponies, your outfit, your saddles, vet fees, and club dues, you are spending thousands of pounds. The only Indians who can afford it are the *maharajas*. Martin lets me use his horses and equipment, and I give him practice and a few pointers."

"Martin is a pig. He hated that you ride so much better than he does. He hated you for teaching him. He tried to get back at you by ordering you to replace the grass. How do you put up with that?"

"By believing I'll be standing on the shore of this country waving good-bye to Banister and everyone like him when they finally sail for England. In the meantime I get to play a game I love. I'm more philosophical than Max, and more patient. Speaking of Max, Rosalind, I want to warn you. Don't let him involve you in some fool scheme in Calcutta. The prince will be surrounded by security guards ready to pounce on anyone who tries to get within an inch of him. You won't like British jails."

"I promise not to take chances," I said, but the truth was, I doubted I could refuse Max.

"I've got to sneak into the club's changing room and get out of these clothes before the members turn up."

Raman left me, and I watched as he glanced both

ways at the entrance to the changing rooms to be sure he wouldn't be seen. I wasn't happy with the way Raman compromised himself, but I did the same, didn't I? The very same club in whose pool I swam and whose parties I went to wouldn't have allowed Raman inside. I resolved not to go there again.

Because we would be in Calcutta for Christmas itself, we celebrated the holiday the night before we left. Ranjit had red poinsettia plants and a small mango tree brought into the sitting room. After dinner, I helped Mother and Aunt Louise decorate the tree with the brightly colored glass ornaments brought over long ago from England. I never lost the excitement of unwrapping the clowns and ballerinas, the kings and queens, nestled in their tissue paper. I forgot from year to year how enchanting they were, each one a memory. Aunt Ethyl stood apart and directed us so that the tree was balanced, the same number of ornaments on one side as the other. There were homemade decorations as well. Against my protests each year, Mother insisted on hanging the gilded paper stars I had made when I was a child.

At the very last we fastened tiny candles into holders,

being careful to place them so that when lit, their flames wouldn't touch anything that could burn. By the time we finished, it was dark out. Father turned off the lights and lit all the candles. We sang carols, Father with his deep bass, Aunt Louise and Aunt Ethyl harmonizing as they seldom did, Mother with her sweet soprano, and me the loudest.

We had all been too excited by news of the prince and busy with our preparations for the trip to Calcutta to give much thought to presents. They had been hastily wrapped and name tags forgotten. Aunt Ethyl was shocked to receive a lacy negligee meant for Mother, while Mother got the double-strength hairnets that Aunt Ethyl had requested from England.

The next day the servants and their families came to see the tree and receive presents that had been thoughtfully chosen by Mother and my aunts. Ranjit was given money to dole out to our servants according to their length of service, as well as rank, which he alone could fathom. Then it was our turn to receive gifts. The owners of Indian stores where we traded and Indian companies who did business with Father's department at the Civil Service came with armfuls of flowers and with boxes of sweet, sticky candies. One man carried an enormous cake with bright pink frosting and, perched on the top, a parakeet in a cage. The moment the man was gone, Aunt Louise opened the cage and washed the frosting from the bird's feet, then off it flew.

There was vacation from tutoring for me and a vacation for my students. Though the boys didn't celebrate Christmas, I had brought sweets as a surprise for the last day of school. The boys had a surprise for me as well.

"You are going to see the son of the royal king," Dev said.

"We made something for you to give the royal prince." Bimal handed me a clumsily wrapped package. For a moment I was afraid he was giving the prince one of his cherished lizards, but the package didn't move. When I unwrapped it, I discovered a crown. It was cleverly made of gold paper, with colored glass pasted on it for jewels.

"I cut it out," Sajala said, "and my brother and the other boys pasted on the glass."

"It's not to wear now," Manu said. "It's to wear when he is king."

"It's lovely," I told them. "Any king would be proud to wear it, but what about the *hartal*?" After all my explaining, did they still not understand what the *hartal* was all about? Did they expect India would have kings forever?

"Oh, we still have the *hartal*," Dev said. "The crown is to wear in England, never here."

So they understood after all. I thought the crown and their message was better than anything Max could give the prince. For a mad moment I saw myself presenting it to the prince, explaining who had made it and where it was to be worn.

The afternoon before we were to leave, when the house was quiet, Max came to fetch me for a walk. "Not now," I pleaded. "I have a million things to do." But this was a serious Max, so unlike him it frightened me into letting everything drop.

The afternoon was unusually warm for December. Our favorite spot along the river would be humid, and the sun striking the water would make a hot glare. In the back of our property, beyond the servants' huts, was a little grove of tamarind trees, and we headed for its shade, passing the little *chota mali*, a goatskin of water slung over his back, watering Mother's English daisies and larkspur and asters that were wilting in the heat of a foreign land. We settled down on a stone ledge, looking around first for snakes, for

111

beyond the ledge was a tangle of overgrown grasses and shrubbery. There was the endless shrill hum of the cicadas high in the trees. A solitary monkey looked down on us from the crown of one of the tamarinds.

"Why all the mystery?" I asked.

"I have something important to ask of you, Rosy. I want you to take it very seriously."

"I always take you seriously, Max. If it weren't for you, I'd still be a foolish girl like the ones at the club with no idea of what's going on in India. You're the one who makes jokes."

"I suppose I make jokes because I always feel that it's not my fight, but the fight of the Indian people. Anyhow, I didn't get you out here in this heat to toss around fine distinctions. There is something you must do when you get to Calcutta."

I had guessed something was coming. Max had been leading up to it for weeks. Now that it was here, I wanted to head back to the house. I wanted my time in Calcutta to be fun. I was looking forward to the parades and parties. "Max, I just want to have a good time. For once I don't want to feel guilty. I'll do what you want when I get back, but let me have a few days to enjoy myself."

I had told him the story of the king's crown Sajala

and the boys had made, and now he turned that against me. "Your students could teach you something. Just read this. It was written by Gandhi for *Young India* last year, and addressed 'The Young Englishman.'" He handed me an envelope, and I extracted a copy of the article.

"Be careful. Don't let anything happen to it. It's meant for the prince."

"I wish that every Englishman in India will see this and give thoughtful attention to it," Gandhi wrote. "Let me introduce myself to you. In my humble opinion no Indian has cooperated with the British Government more than I have for an unbroken period of twenty-nine years of public life...." He told about all the ways he had worked with Great Britain, and then he wrote, "Though my faith in your good intentions is gone, I recognize your bravery, and I know that if you will not yield to justice and reason, you will gladly yield to our bravery." Then Gandhi listed all the injustices in England's rule of India. They made a long and impressive list. He said that if the British wished to end the *hartal*, they had to remove its causes. "You must consider every Indian to be your equal," it read.

"I don't know how the Prince of Wales could resist this," I said.

"First he has to see it, and you are the one to make that possible."

"But, Max, I'm nobody. I'll never get that close to the prince. There has to be someone else, maybe some Indian. I'm sure there will be Indians there."

"Of course there will be a scattering of Indians: *maharajas* and civil servants who owe their jobs to the crown. Do you expect them to risk their jobs and positions? Do you think some major or a general leading the parade would fall out and hand this to the prince? Maybe your father will be the one." Max's voice had taken on the sarcastic tone I hated.

"I'm not stupid, Max. It's just that I don't see how *I* can do it."

"Look, Rosy, you're the perfect one. No one will suspect you. I know you can do it if you set your mind to it. You could charm that monkey down from the tamarind, and behind that pretty face you have a brain that is up for anything. You're my last hope." Gone was the sarcasm. Max was pleading.

Though the envelope in my hand felt as if it might explode at any moment, I couldn't refuse him. "I'll try, Max, but promise not to blame me if I can't do it."

"Rosy, you have to do it. Very few people have a chance to change the course of history. We're all depending on you. It's your chance to act on your beliefs. I know you have the courage."

10

On the day before Christmas, Edward Albert Christian George Andrew Patrick David, the Duke of Cornwall and Prince of Wales, arrived in Calcutta by train. Early that same morning we were preparing to leave by train for the same city. Father treated our journey like one of his military campaigns. Instead of Father, he was Major James. Before we left the house, he lined us up for close inspection, reviewing the troops and sending me in disgrace back to my room to polish my shoes. Our luggage was counted and recounted, and moments before we were to leave he insisted that each one of us produce our ticket. At the train station he would have had us marching in single file but for Mother's plea, "Harlan, this is a pleasure trip."

We squeezed our way onto the crowded train. Many British people had lived all their lives in India and never seen a member of the royal family who ruled them. There was great excitement, as if we were all going on a holiday. Strangers smiled at one another and made pleasant conversation, but Father was concerned only with his little army. He took over a compartment, seated us according to some strict order we didn't understand, and commandeered a *chai wallah* to get us all tea.

The last time I had taken the train from our town to Calcutta, I had been on my way to England and feeling miserable about leaving India. This time the short five-hour trip would have been nothing but excitement and pleasure for me at what was ahead were it not for the envelope I had with me, which was like a coiled snake. What would Father and the other British passengers on the train say if they knew that I carried what they would consider a treasonous message from Gandhi to the Prince of Wales? What would they think if they knew the girl who sat so quietly among them hoped to convince the prince it was time for the British to be sent packing from

India? Most worrying of all, what if Father knew?

The train pulled into Calcutta's busy Howrah Station. For a moment the excitement of the huge station made me forget my worries. Tucked into every corner of the station were Indian families awaiting their train. They made a home of the station; food was prepared and eaten. Children followed the sugarcane *wallah*, begging for a taste of the sweet. The elderly slept on mats, undisturbed in the midst of the confusion. I saw several of the families looking in wonderment at our well-dressed invading army and our piles of baggage, surely wondering how it was possible to possess so much.

There were cries of distress from our fellow passengers as they disembarked from the train. The luggage *wallahs* were all on strike! We were left to stand surrounded by our trunks and suitcases. Father was outraged. "How dare they! And at a time like this. Where are the police? Where is the army?" But all the outrage in the world would not lift our baggage an inch. One by one and with great indignation, people took up their luggage and set out. Father followed suit, managing his own trunk and Mother's, while the rest of us struggled with our suitcases, regretting every extra shoe and shawl we had packed with such disregard for what would happen if we actually had to do our own carrying.

Father commandeered a *tonga*, pausing first to retrieve Aunt Louise, who had escaped to buy steaming *samosas* for an Indian woman and her three little children who looked as if they had not had a meal in days. We traveled down Calcutta's main thoroughfare, Chowringhee Road, to the elegant hotel where Indian doormen who would have nothing to do with the strike fell upon us and our baggage and ushered us inside with many *namastes*. The hotel was all gleaming marble floors and pillars. A Christmas tree decorated in gold and silver ornaments had been set up in the middle of the lobby. Pots of brilliant flowers bloomed. Elegant men and women surged through the lobby, calling to one another on their way to some gala party. I felt I had landed in a storybook and never wanted to turn the page.

Aunt Louise and Aunt Ethyl shared a room, and luxury of all luxuries, I was given my very own tiny room off of Mother and Father's suite. I had a glass door that opened out to a balcony, which looked down on flowing fountains and a blue pool as large as a small lake. I could have perched there forever, but there wasn't a moment to spare. Father was to rehearse with his Second Battalion of the

Gurkha Rifles. Tomorrow his battalion would be a part of the parade to welcome the prince. We were all commandeered to help Father into his uniform, pinning on his medals in the proper order, brushing his *topee*, handing him this and that, and cheering him on as he turned once again from a civil servant into an officer of the British Empire. He looked so handsome that for a moment I forgot all about the message I carried and that it was the British military keeping India under lock and key.

At last he was sent off with a kiss from Mother and cheers from my aunts and myself. Father would be dining with his regiment. Mother had dinner sent up, saying she would have an early night. I joined my aunts in the hotel's elegant dining room, where we had boring British food served with much bowing by turbaned waiters.

Back in my room I was standing on my balcony, longing to escape into the city, when I heard a discreet knock on my door. It was Aunt Louise looking mischievous. "Your Aunt Ethyl is sound asleep. I thought it would be pleasant to go to St. Paul's Cathedral for Christmas Eve services. I do miss London just a bit this time of year."

We thought of walking from the hotel, for we could see the huge white stone cathedral with its square tower ringed round with stone lace. The doorman cautioned us, "You must not walk, Memsahibs," and quickly found us a *tonga*. At once we became a part of the city. The streets were crowded with bicycle *tongas*, horse *tongas*, stray cows, ox carts, men on horseback, and crowds of Indians, the women in colorful *saris* and the men in *salwar kameez*, many wearing the white Congress Party caps. Buildings were decorated with flags and signs welcoming the prince. Here and there a few shops with British names had Christmas decorations in their windows. We also saw signs supporting the *hartal*.

The cathedral was next to the *maidan*, a huge park in the middle of the city. The *tonga* took us through the gardens that surrounded the church and through a cemetery. The cathedral had been built over half a century ago, and many of the gravestones were moss covered, their faded lettering only a sad memory.

Entering the cathedral, we caught our breath, for the entire church was lit with candles. There were candles on every surface. Even the soaring ceilings seemed to glow.

Everywhere you looked were memorials to British soldiers who had died for their country, many of the battles fought in India. On the walls were portraits of the soldiers' faces looking stern and brave. As we stood for a moment in the Chapel of Remembrance for a British officer I saw Aunt Louise wipe away a tear. I didn't know if it was for this man she had never met or if she was thinking that she, too, would one day be buried in a graveyard in India, far from England. I thought of all Father had done in the war to defeat an enemy far away in Mesopotamia and wondered if one day Father's image would appear on the walls of the cathedral, another soldier who had served England bravely.

The familiar Christmas hymns were accompanied by a great organ, its notes shivering through the church. I couldn't concentrate on the sermon. I kept thinking of the memorials. In spite of all my longing for India's freedom, it was hard for me not to feel sympathy for the soldiers who had died in the service of their country. I thought of the letter I had tucked away in my purse, for I was afraid of leaving the letter out of my sight. For a moment I was ashamed to be carrying its message to the prince, for the plea would undo all that these soldiers had fought for. They believed in their dream of an India loyal to England as strongly as I believed in my dream of an India free of England. I wished Max were there to keep my convictions from melting away.

When I told Aunt Louise what I was feeling, without of course mentioning the letter, she said, "You can honor a man for his loyalty, Rosy, but just because he dies for a cause, it doesn't make that cause just."

With so many in the city to see the prince, the Cathedral was filled, and now, with the service over, there was a rush to wave down a *tonga*. I was impatient. The evening was pleasant, and the hotel not far. "Let's walk," I said, and after a moment Aunt Louise agreed. We set off in a thoughtful mood, walking through the cemetery but not pausing. We were eager to leave all the signs of war and death behind.

Once out in the dark streets, we kept our eyes on the lighted hotel only a few blocks away. Every one of the thousands and thousands of Indians living in Calcutta appeared to be out on the street. They paid us hardly any attention, surging by us as if we were no more than moving lampposts or a couple of stray pye-dogs. We clung to each other, afraid one of us would disappear in the darkness and the crowds, never to be seen again.

Some older boys began to follow us like three menacing shadows. They begged us for money. They must have been sixteen or seventeen and Aunt Louise said, "They are too old to be begging like children still." But, she opened her purse, and suddenly the three boys fell upon us. They grabbed at Aunt Louise's purse. I tried to protect her, but they got between us, one boy giving me a hard push that nearly knocked me down. At first Aunt Louise hung on to the purse, indignant and scolding, but they pushed and shoved at her and finally wrenched it free.

They surrounded me, making a grab for my purse. I could smell them and feel their hot breath.

"Rosy, let it go!" Aunt Louise cried, fighting to get to me. "It's only money."

But it wasn't only money. The purse held the message to the prince. I hung on, screaming and kicking, until one of the boys put a hand over my mouth and gave me a hard slap. My cheek stung. Another boy twisted my hair. Still I clung to my purse with both hands. I kicked at them and bit the hand that covered my mouth. The boy yelped with pain and struck me so hard I fell.

Aunt Louise had worked free and ran in the street calling for help. Two distinguished Indian men, one with gray hair and the other younger and wearing a Congress hat, fell upon the boys with their umbrellas, scolding the thieves as if they were five-year-olds. To escape the blows, the boys ran off, taking Aunt Louise's purse with them.

The men now seemed as angry with us as they had been with the thieves. The older man said, "Memsahibs, whatever are you about, wandering in the streets at this time of evening?" He helped me up. My dress was ripped, and one knee badly scrapped and bleeding. The Congress hat man tried to comfort Aunt Louise, who was trembling.

"We were just on our way from St. Paul's to our hotel," I said. I looked down to be sure my purse was still there, as if I couldn't believe the feel of it in my clasped hands, hands I was sure I could never unclench.

As if we were at a reception the older man formally introduced himself, "I am Mr. Sastri, and this is Mr. Brose. You are unwise to travel these streets at night and make of yourselves a temptation."

I was indignant. My knee hurt, and I was sure I was missing some hair. I could still taste the hand that I had bit into. "It wasn't our fault!"

Aunt Louise hastily cut in. "We are so grateful," she said. "I don't know how we can thank you."

"Not at all," Mr. Brose said. "I am sorry you have had so frightening an experience. I hope you will not judge our city by this little misadventure."

"It wasn't just a misadventure," I said. "They could have hurt us."

Mr. Brose looked down at my purse. "Perhaps it was unwise not to give them your money. Had you done that there would have been no violence."

"I urged her to," Aunt Louise said.

"I don't see why I should willingly hand over my money to the first person who wants to take it."

"Quite right," Mr. Sastri said, smiling for the first time. "You were as brave as you were foolish. Now, just to avoid any further unpleasantness, you must allow us to escort you back to your hotel."

We made an odd little parade. Aunt Louise, her hat tipped at a roguish angle, clung to Mr. Brose, and I marched behind Mr. Sastri, my hair falling in a tangle, my dress torn, and blood trickling down my leg. My only thought was to make sure Aunt Louise kept our adventure to herself and then to scurry to my room and clean up before my parents saw us, but luck was against us. Just as we reached the safety of the hotel, Father's *tonga* drew up.

Father jumped from the *tonga*, and the next minute he was shouting at our rescuers. "Who are you? What have you done! I'll have the police on you!"

At once Aunt Louise, who had pulled herself together at the sight of my father, interrupted him.

"Harlan, we were set upon by some young thieves, and these gentlemen kindly came to our rescue. They chased off our assailants at great danger to themselves. If you will just come inside, Rosy and I will tell you exactly what happened." She turned to Mr. Sastri and Mr. Brose, who had grasped their umbrellas with firm hands at Father's furious accusations. I was sure they were mightily sick of us by now.

"I'm afraid we have given you a great deal of trouble," Aunt Louise apologized. "I can't begin to thank you enough."

I was upset by Father jumping to conclusions and sorry I had not shown more gratitude. "Yes, thank you so much," I said, and offered my hand to each of the men in turn. Solemnly, they shook it.

Father apologized. "I am sorry. I'm afraid I jumped to conclusions."

"Yes," Mr. Sastri said, "you see your daughter with two Indian gentlemen."

Father had the grace to blush.

"You are here to see the prince?" Mr. Brose asked.

"Yes, my battalion of the Gurkha Rifles will be in the parade."

"What an honor for you," Mr. Sastri said without an ounce of sarcasm. "Let us give you our cards." They bowed to us, then melded with the crowd.

"Who are they?" I asked.

Father studied the cards. "They both appear to be lawyers. All very regular, but that one chap was wearing a Congress Party cap. I don't like that. Still, they seemed decent enough. Now for the two of you." And Father led us to our rooms and all but locked us in. Alone, I stood looking out from my balcony at the city that was now forbidden to me.

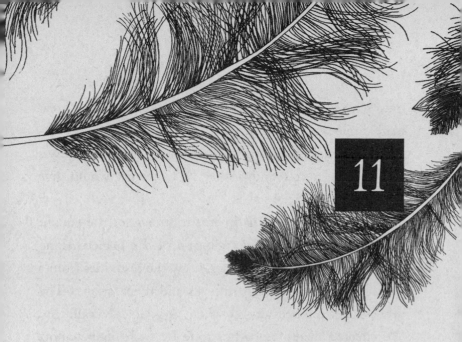

11

At last we were to see the prince, and Father was to have his moment of glory. The prince was to drive in state to the Victoria Memorial. There he would preside at its official opening and be introduced by the Bengal governor, the Earl of Ronaldshay, whose speech was decorated by my own Mr. Snartwell. Father and his battalion of Gurkhas would join other battalions in the parade. I had seen the memorial with Mother while it was still being built. It was set in the middle of the *maidan*. I thought the white marble memorial, two hundred feet high, looked like a monstrous birthday cake. Around its dome were figures meant to represent, among other things, justice, which must have seemed ironic to the citizens of India. The great marble pile was built to honor Queen Victoria and to display scenes and mementoes of her life. Queen Victoria was the prince's great-grandmother, and his visit would give the memorial official status.

Thousands of Indians lined the streets for the parade, shoving and pushing for a glimpse of the prince. Along with my aunts and my mother, I saw the festivities from a stand reserved for British officials and their families. The procession stretched almost as far as your eye could see. We cheered madly as Father rode by with his battalion. I thought he looked years younger and guessed he was imagining himself riding into battle for some great cause.

All at once, shouts rang out and there was the prince, splendid in his dress uniform, rather slight and rather shy looking. Walking a little behind him on the red carpet was a naval officer in his navy whites who looked rather more the way a prince should. As they reached the entrance a little boy ran toward the prince. At once the police closed in, but the child only wanted to present the prince with a kitten as a gift. I gave the prince points for thanking the child nicely, though His Royal Highness did not touch the kitten, but let an aide take it. In such crowds it was

impossible to hear the prince's speech, but from the enthusiastic cheers I gathered Mr. Snartwell's additions were a
great success.

We just had time to rush back to the hotel and change
into our afternoon dresses for the garden party at Government House. Our dresses were of floral printed chiffon,
light and flowing. With the dresses we wore white gloves
right up to our elbows and large floppy hats. As Father
helped us climb into the *tonga* we had to duck around one
another's hats, and once we got going we had to hold on
to them to keep them from flying off. As always, clutched
in my hands was my purse, with the letter inside.

There was a long reception line, with the prince at the
end like a prize. Father bowed and we curtsied our way
down the line. The men were in gray tailcoats and top hats
or dress uniforms, but the prince was in a kilt and wearing
a Glengarry hat with a fetching bit of ribbon attached to
it. There were Indian guests as well, the men in perfectly
tailored *salwar kameez*, the women in richly embroidered
silk *saris*. On the women's arms were bracelets of gold.
These were the wealthy Indians, officials and even a few
maharajas. There were fewer Indian women than men, for
more traditional women were not seen in public.

As I was nearing the prince I considered for a desperate moment thrusting the letter at him like the child had handed him the kitten, but Max had given me strict instructions that I was not to do that. The prince would only hand it to a personal attendant, as he had handed off the kitten. The equerry would never let him see it. I had to find a way of making sure he read it.

I was nearly to the prince when I looked up to see the handsome naval officer. He introduced himself as Lord Louis Mountbatten. I flushed as I put my gloved hand in his. He held it for what seemed longer than the usual few seconds and asked me to repeat my name. I then moved on, following Father, who bowed to the prince, and Mother and my aunts and I all bobbed up and down in curtsies. The prince had nice blue eyes and a pleasant smile, but he didn't really look at you as if he saw you. Instead, he looked a little weary, as if he were reading a book he had read many times and hadn't much liked in the first place.

Once we were released from the formality of the reception line, we were free to wander about the gardens. Servants in white uniforms and turbans passed a democratic mix of refreshments—cucumber sandwiches and crisp samosas. Father headed for the other officers. Mother and my aunts spotted Mrs. Snartwell who looked ravishing in her elegant hand-me-down, with her red hair all in curls. I had just started to go join them when the reception line broke up and Lord Louis made his way to me. Father had told me that Lord Louis, though he was only twenty, a couple of years younger than the prince, was serving as an equerry, a personal attendant as well as a sort of companion to the prince. They were cousins, both having Queen Victoria as their great-grandmother.

"You look as bored as I am," Lord Louis said.

"How can you be bored traveling with the Prince of Wales?"

"Oh, David is nice enough, but it's what we have to do. Yesterday was Christmas day, and we were plowed under with gifts and cards of good wishes. It'll be my job to write thank-you notes for them. And tomorrow we must go on a paper chase."

"A paper chase!"

"Yes, there's no fox hunting here, and David has to have his riding. Two hundred grown-up men gallop over fences and across ditches following a paper trail someone has laid down."

I don't know how I found the courage, but knowing what Max would have said, I asked, "How can the prince learn anything about India if he just keeps with his own people? Isn't he interested in the Indian people? Doesn't he want to know about the country?"

"The country hasn't been very welcoming, you know. These strikes and signs and all that rubbish. Not very hospitable if you ask me. I would think the Indian people would be happy to have the Prince of Wales here."

That was too much for me. "That just shows how little you know. The Indian people want their freedom."

"Oh, I say! You're not a Bolshie or anything? Or one of those awful Gandhiists?" He looked quickly around to be sure no one had overheard me.

I lowered my voice. "There can't be anything wrong with wanting to rule your own country."

"Eventually, of course. But the Indians are like children, and you can't let children run things."

"That's the most stupid thing I've ever heard. The Indians had a splendid empire while the British were still running around in animal skins."

I was afraid he would call for the police, who lurked behind every bush in the garden. Instead he laughed.

"You're as bad as Edwina. She's always going on like that. What would you have us do?"

He wasn't angry with me. Maybe he did care, and he was certainly close to the prince. He called him David. "There is something you could do, if you would."

"Try me."

I looked around to be sure no one could hear us, but the other guests were all in pods, chattering to one another or grouped adoringly around the prince. "I've been entrusted with an important letter for the prince. It was written by Gandhi."

"You can't be serious? How on earth did you get your hands on a thing like that?"

"Someone I'm friendly with writes for *Young India*, a magazine that Gandhi started. I was the only person who would be at all near the prince, the only person my friend knew he could trust."

"But there are Indian guests here at the garden party."

"First of all, the only Indians invited were those the government felt to be friendly to the British, and even if an Indian guest who supported Gandhi came, he would be arrested if he stuck a letter like that under the nose of the Prince of Wales. The thing is, I can't give it to him either

135

because one of his flunkeys"—I saw Lord Louis wince—
"sorry, I mean one of his equerries, would just take it and
keep it so the prince would never see it. I need to give it
to someone I trust who would see that he got it." I took
a deep breath. "Someone like you, if I could just convince
you that Gandhi is right."

Lord Louis stood looking at me. Finally, he said, "I'm
afraid you will never convince me of that, but I might pass
the letter along to David if you do a favor for me."

"Yes, just tell me what it is."

"The thing is, I have a girlfriend, Edwina, and she is
marvelous. She's right here in India, though not here in
Calcutta. We want to be engaged, but my family thinks
I'm too young. Besides, they think because I'm related to
the royal family I ought to marry a European princess so
I can have my own country to rule. I don't want to rule a
country, and I don't want to marry anyone but Edwina."

"I think that's all so romantic."

"Well, the thing is, they're doing everything to keep us
apart, and I'm determined to see Edwina before I go back
to England. I need to throw them off the track. I thought if
I looked like I was enjoying myself with another girl, they
wouldn't be so suspicious."

"If I say yes, you would promise to give the letter to the Prince of Wales?"

"I absolutely promise on my dead great-grandmother's grave."

Queen Victoria! It couldn't be difficult to spend a day or two with someone as pleasant and as handsome as Lord Louis, even if he didn't understand anything about India. Maybe I could even teach him something. "I'll do it," I said. And that was how I spent the rest of my time in Calcutta with my own royal escort.

12

That evening, Lord Louis was waiting for me at the formal ball. "No more Lord Louis," he said. "My friends call me Dickie." He swept me onto the dance floor. "I don't suppose you are going to lecture me about that little man in a loincloth all the while we are dancing?"

"Of course I am. You have so much to learn. Gandhi is wearing just a loincloth because he objects to Indians having to buy British cloth."

"I notice you aren't following in his footsteps. What do you do when you aren't going about being a spy?"

"I have my own school. The *hartal* has closed all the government schools, so the Congress Party has started up its own schools. They let me have one too, because they know I am on their side. I have five boys, and a girl who listens."

"Who *listens*?"

"Well, in India girls aren't encouraged to be educated."

"That's one up for the British. Girls go to school in England. Well, to be honest, they aren't welcome in the best colleges, but Edwina was shipped off to school when she was practically a toddler. Anyhow, if you close all your schools, where are your leaders going to come from?"

I didn't like being on the defensive, especially in the middle of a ballroom, with music playing and Dickie purposely dancing in circles to make me dizzy. I asked, "Suppose Germany had won the last war and marched into England and told everyone what to do and wouldn't let any Englishmen have a say in their own government. How would you like that?"

The music stopped, and Dickie said, "I can't think and march you around. Let's go out on the veranda and get some air. You're wearing that airy thing, but this formal uniform is hot as blazes."

I saw my aunts watching our escape, Aunt Louise with a smile, Aunt Ethyl with a raised eyebrow. There were other looks in our direction. Dickie noticed them as well.

"Excellent," he said, "they're beginning to gossip about us. Just what I hoped."

"But what about *my* reputation? I suppose you think I should be grateful to be seen with you. What, exactly, are you doing on the trip?" I had seen the envious looks on the faces of several girls, but I wasn't going to give Dickie any satisfaction.

"I'm just along on the trip to keep the prince jolly. He gets into the most awful moods. I can tell you he doesn't like the strike, or *hartal* as you call it. He thinks it very rude."

"His visit here in India caused nearly three thousand Indians to be arrested," I said. "They were dragged from their homes and put in jail just so your prince wouldn't have to be bothered by demonstrations. How rude is that?"

"He's not my prince, as you call him, and the only reason Gandhi himself wasn't put in prison is that the prince is here. You have the prince to thank for that. The authorities didn't want a lot of unpleasant news coming out about Gandhi doing one of his starvings while David was in the country. What's more, I happen to know that India's viceroy, Lord Reading, offered Gandhi a chance for India one day to be a part of the Commonwealth like Canada and Australia. He was foolish to refuse."

"He doesn't want India to be a part of anything. He wants India's independence."

"Look here, Rosalind, if I have to spend all my time with you nattering away on politics, the agreement's off. Can't we just agree to disagree and have a good time? I feel like I'm back at university again, and I didn't much like it the first time."

So I relented. We went back to the dance floor. The other men must have wondered what Dickie found so interesting in me, especially since he was older, and they began to cut in to see for themselves. I liked the attention but none of them were nearly as attractive as Dickie, even with all his stupid ideas. Then, almost at the end of the dance, I saw His Royal Highness, Edward Albert Christian George Andrew Patrick David, the Duke of Cornwall and Prince of Wales, heading toward Dickie and me. Dickie saw him too.

"Here is your chance, my girl, to hand over your letter and see if David will have you thrown in jail."

My letter was at the hotel under my mattress. It had never occurred to me to bring it to a ballroom.

"May I?" the prince said. "I don't see why you should monopolize this young lady, Dickie." He took me in his royal arms. "I am sure I had the pleasure of greeting you in the reception line, but I'm afraid there were so many people. . . ."

"Rosalind James, sir. My father led a battalion of Gurkha Rifles during the war." His hand was light on my waist, but we glided easily about the ballroom in spite of my feeling so nervous that my feet were like two wooden sticks. Over his shoulder I could see the incredulous look on the face of Aunt Ethyl.

"Very commendable. England owes much to men like your father. I only saw a bit of the war. In spite of my pleading they kept me out of action, afraid the enemy would kidnap me and cause a lot of fuss. I've noticed that you seem to have cast some kind of spell on Dickie. I have seldom seen him so devoted."

I blushed, wondering if he suspected Dickie's attention to me was just to keep people from knowing how much he cared for Edwina.

He laughed at my confusion, "Oh, I'm in on the plot. Dickie tells me he is to do you a favor as well. I suppose next time you come to London you want to be presented to my father."

I had seen pictures of girls in long white dresses with a train and ostrich feathers in their hair lined up to curtsy to the sovereign at the beginning of the social season. After the presentation, you backed out of the room. I couldn't imagine myself doing that without falling on my face. "Oh, no, I couldn't see myself wearing ostrich feathers." And then, forgetting that one never discussed politics with the royal family, I said, "I had hoped to . . ." But then Dickie cut back in and took a firm hold on me.

"Sorry, David, the governor has asked if you would join him. He has some *maharaja* or other dying to press the royal palm."

The prince made a little bow, thanked me for the dance, and left us.

Dickie said, "Your face got all flushed, and I could tell you were about to make an awful fool of yourself, and I thought I had better rescue you. Give me the letter for him if you must, but spare him one of your lectures. Now I'm all hot and tired of dancing. Let's go wade in the fountain."

We paused on the veranda to take off our shoes and stockings, which we hid in a pot of poinsettias, and then we wandered barefoot across the soft grass to the fountain. We sat there in the moonlight with our feet in the cool water and the music playing in the distance, thinking our own thoughts. It was such a romantic evening, and I wondered if Dickie was missing Edwina. For myself, in my mind I was rehearsing how I would tell Max I had danced with the Prince of Wales.

We were both watching a small frog splashing about in the fountain and exchanging smiles at its antics when suddenly a night heron, its great wings spread out, glided down from a tree, snatched the little frog in its beak, and flew off with it. Dickie and I looked at each other, shocked. It was only a frog, and the night heron had been so gorgeous sifting down in the night, but it seemed an omen. I felt all the pleasure we had in the evening fade away. Why should we be enjoying ourselves while men were in prison for no reason but their wish to free their country?

Silently, we walked back and retrieved our shoes and stockings and joined the others. Father was waiting for me. He had a pleasant word for Dickie and then announced, "Rather a long day. I believe we will make our excuses. Come along, Rosy."

As we made our way outside, Aunt Ethyl said, "I never thought I would live to see the day a niece of mine danced with the Prince of Wales. I hope you showed him the proper courtesy."

"You made a lovely couple," Aunt Louise said. "It was like something in a story book."

Mother asked, "What in the world did you talk about?"

"I told him Father led a battalion of Gurkhas during the war."

Father looked pleased. "And what did he say to that, Rosy?"

"He said that was very commendable."

"Did he indeed? It was good of you to mention my service during the war, Rosy, and of course those of my Gurkhas. We mustn't forget them. Many of them sacrificed their lives."

But the prince had said nothing of that.

We all crowded into one *tonga* to travel through the dark Calcutta streets, where the homeless lay sleeping on the sidewalks, the lucky with quilts to lie upon. Aunt Ethyl was the first to speak. "You spent rather a lot of time with Lord Louis, Rosalind. Some of the women remarked about it. One even asked if there was anything between the two of you."

"Of course there isn't," Father said. "She is just a child, but nothing wrong with Lord Louis. His father was Britain's First Sea Lord. Terrible shame he got pitched out."

"What do you mean 'pitched out'?" I asked.

Aunt Ethyl said, "He had to resign. The family name, before they changed it to Mountbatten, was Battenberg. You couldn't have someone with connections to the German royal family heading the British navy while Britain fought the Germans."

"It was very unfair," Aunt Louise said. "No one could have been more loyal, and he had nothing to do with the Germans."

"Of course not," Father said. "As for your young friend, Rosy, he served very credibly in our navy as a midshipman during the war."

"And his grandmother was the daughter of Queen Victoria," Mother said. "There is no reason Rosalind can't enjoy his company."

I could see Mother already had me married and moving into a palace. I wondered what they would think if they knew about Edwina and the letter under my mattress.

The next day, while Mother and my aunts were busy in shops and at a reception at the Calcutta Club, and Father renewed acquaintances with his army buddies, Dickie took me to see a polo match in the morning and a paper chase in the afternoon. The paper chase consisted of one group on horseback laying a trail of paper across high mud walls and deep ditches for the second group of riders to follow at the risk of their necks, and sure enough, horses and riders were falling in heaps. I thought it the most stupid exercise I had ever seen and told Dickie so. There was another garden party at Government House, this time to honor *maharajas* from nearby princely states. The *maharajas* live in luxury in their palaces under the protection of the British crown. The turbans and gold belts of the *maharajas* were stuck with emeralds and rubies, their jackets were of heavy silk and their swords encrusted with jewels. A few of them were accompanied by their *maharanees* magnificent in saris lavishly embroidered with gold thread, but many of the *maharajas'* wives had entered into *purdah* and were confined to their *zenana*, never to be seen by any male other than a close relative.

Looking at all that showy splendor I accused Dickie, "You and the prince are supposed to be here to see India. You don't see anything but the backs of horses and stupid garden parties and dances. You don't know any Indians except the *maharajas*."

"It's not my fault. We go where we are told. What

would you have us do? Wander the streets?"

"That's exactly what you ought to do." On a sudden impulse I said, "Let me show you."

A smile was spreading over Dickie's face. "And the prince, too?"

My imagination had not reached that far, but I felt the fate of the India rested in my hands. Rather than just handing the prince a letter about India, wouldn't it be better to let him see what India was suffering?

"Yes, the prince, too. Do you think he would come?"

"I can tell you David is bored to death. He would do anything to escape, but no one, absolutely no one must know and you must not use this as an opportunity to push the letter in his face."

"How will you ever manage it?"

"Leave it to me. You're not the only one capable of cloak and dagger secrets. The party is over at four. I'll catch up with you just outside of your hotel at five and I'll bring David if he's up for it. I don't promise anything, but you will have me. And don't breathe a word to a soul! Now away with you, I need to talk with David."

I was back in my hotel room, breathless. I tore off my fancy clothes with trembling hands and pulled on the plain skirt and blouse I had worn on the train where good clothes weren't worn because of the soot coming in the windows. I combed out my curls and twisted them into a simple braid. I didn't risk a purse, knowing that would be a temptation where we were going. And though I could not believe the prince would come, I thought of the letter under my mattress, but I left it there, remembering my promise to Dickie. Then I sneaked, quiet as a shadow, out of my room and took the elevator to the lobby.

13

I didn't really think Dickie would appear, and I certainly didn't believe the prince would come; still, I was disappointed when I walked out of the hotel and Dickie wasn't there. I saw no one but a doorman chasing away some beggars, and, standing on the walkway, two Sikhs in white *salwar kameez*, their heads wrapped in their traditional turbans, turbans that covered their hair, which they never cut. Sikhs had their own admirable religion. They believed in the brotherhood of man and were against the caste system, supporting equal rights for everyone. They were a devout lot who had a hard time of it in wars, because of their peaceful nature.

So why were these two Sikhs arguing? I looked again. Enveloped in the turbans were the heads of Dickie and His Royal Highness. The tans they had acquired playing polo, going on paper chases, and hunting tigers made them the same golden brown as any Indian. I looked quickly around, but no one seemed to be paying them attention. The doorman came up to me. "May I get a *tonga* for you, Memsahib?"

"No, thank you. I think I will walk a bit." He frowned, but I moved quickly away from the hotel. The two Sikhs followed. When we were out of sight of the doorman, Dickie caught up with me. "Well, here we are."

I turned to the prince. "Oh, sir, are you sure this is all right?"

"Of course it isn't. If I were discovered, it would cause a great scandal, and you must call me David. Now where shall we go?"

Only a short distance from the hotel we were already swallowed up by hundreds of people pushing their way past us. Beggar children had spotted me and were pulling at my dress. On the street, bicycle and horse *tongas* made their way around bullock carts and the occasional wandering cow. Dickie cursed as filthy sewage water that ran along the curb splashed on his white trousers.

In another city we might have seemed out of place, but a block from the hotel we were just three people among a million all crowded together like grains in a sack of rice. Calcutta swallowed us up in one great gulp. The crowds pushed us onto the street, where we were nearly overrun by *tonga wallahs* who cursed us for getting in their way. Only a few days before, David had traveled this same street in a magnificent coach pulled by six white horses and cheered by thousands.

We pushed our way back onto the sidewalk, and now we were beset by beggars who snatched at us, plucking at David's jacket. Shopkeepers bounded out of their stalls to urge us to buy. "Very old ivory." "Gold bracelets for the lady." David, looking hot under his heavy turban, asked for a cold drink of *shikanji* and was embarrassed to find he had no money to pay. Dickie reached into his pocket. "Royals never carry money," he explained.

We passed Dalhouse Square, walked by Calcutta's enormous post office, and turned toward the Hooghly River to find ourselves in another world. There were hundreds of small shacks constructed of bamboo, thatch, cardboard, bits of straw matting, or just mud. They were nothing but cubbyholes; still, the people with a bit of shelter were the lucky ones. Hundreds stretched out on the ground with no protection against the hot sun, some so weak and motionless you could not be sure they were alive. The canals flowed from the river like fingers on a hand. Dickie gave me a disgusted look. "What's that smell?"

"There aren't sewers here. It all flows into the canals and the river."

He looked at the men bathing in the canals, and the women slapping clothes against the walls of the canal. An old man with no legs crawled along the filthy sidewalk toward David, his hand out. A woman in tatters lifted her crying child to Dickie. A leper with no nose snatched at my skirt, tearing it in her eagerness for my attention and money. I saw a child whose limbs were twisted into hideous shapes, and I thought of Nadi. Even knowing where it would end up, I gave him my last *anna*. When they saw we had no more money to give, the beggars turned on us with curses.

David and Dickie lagged behind me. At last I took mercy on them and led them to the *maidan*, where we settled gratefully under a grove of mango trees. A noisy woodpecker was after beetles. A monkey plucked a green mango and lobbed it at us. The police kept the park clear of beggars, and even the wild dogs that were everywhere in the city stayed away. The *maidan* was meant for the British, but since I accompanied the two Sikhs, nothing was said.

"That is your India," David said.

"No, that is *your* India," I answered. "What do you think of it?"

"I don't know how people live in such misery. It's hopeless."

"No. It's not hopeless. Why can't there be homes and schools and water taps?" I was building a dream right before our eyes.

David said, "Do you think if every Englishman left tomorrow, the next day this would be a paradise?"

"Maybe not, but I believe it would be less a hell."

"You're too much an optimist," Dickie said.

"I couldn't live with myself if I thought nothing could get better."

David said, "I can't say I'm grateful for this afternoon."

Was he angry with me? Hadn't any of it made a difference? Had I just made a fool of myself? I was disappointed and angrier with myself than with David and Dickie. I snapped at them, "Doubtless you would rather have spent the afternoon playing polo or going on a paper chase."

Dickie looked shocked, but David reached over and put his royal hand on mine, startling me. "Not at all. You're too quick to judge. All you see is what you want to see. This official trip of mine hasn't been one happy round of polo or pig sticking. I have sweltered, buttoned up to the neck in a miserable uniform, reviewing countless troops. I have suffered through one garden party after another, saying inane things to boring people. I sat through interminable dinners in *maharajas'* palaces. I am doing all of this for the purpose of bringing India and Britain closer. Now you rub my imperial nose in all there is still to do. It isn't as if we have given India nothing, you know. India has an excellent train system that has opened up its country. It has a fine postal service, an army, a police force."

"Yes, all supervised by the British. What difference does a postal system make if you can't write, or a railway if you've no money to travel, or an army or police force if they are ordered to arrest or shoot at India's own people?" I stopped, alarmed to hear myself speaking this way to the king's son.

Dickie was clearly upset with me. "Rosy, you have to be fair. It's not all David's fault."

"No, it's not my fault, but I owe you a debt of gratitude. We thought this would be a kind of lark, our masquerade just a joke, but it turned out to be something quite different. I can't say I'm grateful, but I shan't forget it. I don't believe you are right to want us to hand India its freedom, but you have given me something to think about. Now, let's see you back to your hotel."

"And, Rosalind," Dickie said, "I must have your word that you will never tell anyone about these last hours."

I gave my word at once, though I would have given everything to be able to tell Max. In moments we were back on Chowringee Road, David and Dickie now much the worse for wear, their turbans lopsided, their white trousers grass stained, and I had to hold together the tear in my skirt.

At the hotel the doorkeeper took one look at us and cried out, "Oh, Memsahib, you have been set upon again! Oh, what will your family say! Let me call the police on these thieves." He had a whistle at his lips, and I had a vision of His Royal Highness in an Indian prison.

"No, no. They are friends. They just brought me back to the hotel."

The doorman looked doubtful, but Dickie and David

did not wait to be sure he was convinced. They leapt into a *tonga* and melted into the crowded street.

Father saw me before I could escape to my room. "Rosalind, look at you. Where in the world have you been? I hope you are not involving yourself with that element that seeks to overthrow the British monarchy in India."

"Oh no, Father. I absolutely am not. On the contrary."

"Don't be pert with me, young lady. Just what do you mean?"

Quickly, I said, "I was with Dickie, Lord Louis, and he's Queen Victoria's great-grandson, isn't he? So I was supporting the monarchy."

"I don't wish to be critical of Queen Victoria," Father said. "It would be the last thing to enter my head, but there have been a few rather odd offsprings of the queen along the way. I had thought Lord Louis was quite sound."

"Oh, yes. We just happened to get crushed in a bit of a crowd."

"One of his competitive polo matches, I suppose. Now go tidy up. We are due at the Brazelhursts' reception for the prince in an hour. Tomorrow, I'm pleased to say, we leave for home."

Alone in my room, I went over the last hours. Had

I made any difference? Or had I done harm by showing David all the suffering? Would I have done better to have him meet the well-educated Indian leaders who could have spoken to him about India's problems in the language of Oxford and Cambridge, where many of them were educated? Probably he would never have agreed to such a meeting. It was David's purpose to bring England and India closer in order to make India accept England's rule; Gandhi's purpose was the exact opposite.

That afternoon as I made my way down the reception line, I paused when I got to Dickie, as if to chat for a moment, then dropped my purse. As he reached down to pick it up for me I handed him Gandhi's letter.

"You've kept your bargain," he said. "I'll keep mine, and I'll keep my eye on you. I want to know what you are up to."

When I came to David, I managed a curtsy, but my hand was trembling as he took it. What if he called the police and had me thrown in jail as a revolutionary?

"Ah, Miss James," he said, "I want you to know that I will never think of India without thinking of you. Perhaps one day you will come to England and wear those white feathers." He smiled as he pressed my hand.

14

Max and Raman were at our door minutes after our *tonga* brought us home from the train. "How did you know when I would be back?" They led me into the garden, where the three of us settled on a bench, displacing two lizards and a bright orange bug.

Max said, "I was covering a Congress Party meeting for the magazine and ran into Aziz, who had heard it from his wife, Isha, who knew about it from her mother, Amina, who does for your mother. Never mind all that. Just tell us. Did you get the letter to the prince?"

"Yes. I gave it to Dickie, who gave it to the prince."

"Dickie? Who's Dickie? How could you possibly

rely on someone whose name is Dickie?"

"Actually, Dickie's name is Louis Frances Albert Victor Nicholas George Mountbatten, and he's the great-grandson of Queen Victoria and the prince's best friend on the trip."

Raman asked, "So how did you get to be such pals with this fellow?"

I was enjoying myself. "Oh, we just hit it off. Actually, I saw quite a bit of him. He promised to give it to David, I mean the prince."

"David!" Max said. "Now I know you're making fools of us. I'll bet you didn't get within fifty feet of the prince."

"A lot closer than that. I danced with him." How I relished the looks of astonishment and disbelief on their faces.

Raman said, "You mean the prince just asked you to dance?"

"I don't believe a word of it," came a murmur from Max.

"I don't care whether you believe me or not."

"Did you give him the letter?" Max asked.

"On the dance floor? Of course not. I didn't carry it about with me to dances. Whether you believe me or not, Dickie gave it to him. He gave me his word, and I believe him."

Max said. "I don't see how you could have trusted this Dickie person, but I'll take your word for it. We'll see what comes of it, but you were as likely to dance with the prince as I was. You're just playing games with us. Now tell us all about Calcutta."

I told them about the parades and parties and receptions.

"Just as I thought," Raman said. "The prince would never have had a chance to see the real India. What a pity. You may believe you got that letter to him, but I doubt he read it."

"And exactly what were you doing with this Mountbatten fellow?" Max asked. "How could you be interested in someone related to Queen Victoria?"

"Actually, Dickie was very nice. We spent a lot of time together, and you can be sure I talked to him about freedom for India."

Max was skeptical. "I suppose while you were waltzing around together you told him how his people had their boot on the neck of India."

"I didn't put it quite as charmingly as you do, but I told him."

"And did he listen to you?" Raman asked.

"Yes, he did. I think you would have liked him,

Raman; he was very good at polo. So was the prince."

"What a pity I wasn't there to play a *chukker* or two with them."

"We haven't come to hear about polo," Max said. "What did you learn about the political situation? What did they have to say about the *hartal*?"

"Oh, there was no talk of the *hartal* at the polo matches and the dances."

In spite of their pounding me with questions, I refused to say more, and they went away puzzled. I had to keep my word to Dickie and David, but I longed to tell them how we spent the afternoon. How I would have loved to see their faces when they heard that.

After Max and Raman left, I went to see Hari, though I still thought of him as Nadi. I had decided that I would do all I could to help Hari grow up to become a great leader of his country, someone who could explain India to the British. He would go to a good school, and if the schools were still closed, I would instruct him myself.

Safia greeted me as she always did. She was polite but watchful, never fully trusting me, afraid I might try to take Hari away. Hari was always glad to see me, but with each visit I saw that he had less and less interest in me and my

English instruction and was eager to be off to splash about in the water or catch frogs with the other children.

"Safia, let me have him to myself for an afternoon. It's difficult to instruct him here. He sees the other children playing, and he wants to be with them. Already, in just the few days I have been gone, he has forgotten the words I taught him last time."

"What good are the English words you give him," Safia asked. "Who but you will he say them to?"

"Your son can be a great man, a great leader of his people, but he must know the English words so he can explain India to the English."

"Why don't the Englishmen learn Hindi like you did?"

I didn't know what to say to that. "Safia, don't you want your son to be important?"

She looked puzzled. "Hari is important."

"Yes, of course, but that's not what I mean. He could be a great leader of his people. He could go to England to school."

Safia was alarmed. "England? That is very far."

"Well, of course I don't mean now. When he is grown-up." I could hear the urgency in my voice. So could Safia. She would be afraid that if I didn't get my way, I would try to take Hari away. I'm ashamed to think I let her believe that, I was so in love with my idea of Hari being the one to bring India its freedom. Reluctantly, she agreed.

After that, instead of teaching Hari English at his home, I went twice a week to take him with me for the afternoon. Aunt Louise was delighted to see him, asking only, "Are you sure, Rosy, that this is all right with Safia?" I assured her it was.

Aunt Ethyl only said, "You must give him a good bath, Rosalind, if you plan to bring him into the house."

I was so insulted I refused to take Hari inside but arranged our lessons in a shady part of the garden, spreading out a quilt and bringing toys for him to name and treats to ask for in English. It was there that Raman found us. He knew about Hari and how he had been rescued.

Raman settled down with us. "What have we here? I thought this child was back with his parents."

I explained to Raman that I wanted to teach Hari English and that I also wanted him to learn how to be comfortable with the British. "I want him to go to Cambridge like you did and then return home and be a great leader of India, someone who can speak to the British in a way that will make them listen."

"You want to turn him into a little Englishman?"

"No, of course not. I just want him to be on equal terms with Englishmen. I want them to respect him."

"You think Englishmen will not respect an Indian? If you do, whose fault is that, and why should you be a part of it?"

"When you came home from Cambridge, you were like an Englishman."

"Yes, and I paid for it. I had lost my identity. I was neither Indian nor British. I was an impostor. I won't let you do that to Hari."

"What do you mean?"

"I mean if you try to turn him into something he isn't, he will never be happy, and the British will never respect him. You must be who you are. That is the only way to be happy. Who is the Indian most respected by the British? Who in India has the most power against the British?"

"Gandhi."

"Of course, and with his loincloth, his spinning wheel, his refusal to avail himself of any luxury the British offer him, no one could be more Indian and less British."

"But it was in England that he trained to be a lawyer."

"Yes, but he has put all that behind him. I don't say

Hari should not one day go to university in England, but let him go as he is. Let him go as an Indian and let him come back an Indian, not an imitation Englishman. He is an Indian after all."

I was crushed. Raman was right. I had fallen into the trap of thinking only someone who was like the British would impress the British. If the English were to accept India as an equal, they must accept Indians as equals. "Raman, I don't know what I was thinking. It was stupid. I'm sorry."

"Yes, it was. Now let's give this poor child who at the great age of three years can't recite a single line by Shakespeare some fun."

The rest of the afternoon was spent with the three of us playing hide-and-seek among the acacia trees and the fragrant gardenia shrubs.

15

Now that I held my classes for the boys out of doors, Sajala was an accepted member of the group. Because she was a few years older, she was quick to learn, and I had taken to giving her more difficult work than I gave the boys. She was always fearful her parents would find out about her attending class and had made Dev promise to keep her secret.

Sajala told me, "When Mother saw me with Dev's book, she said I would do better to spend my time improving my making of *puri* and my *chapatis*. Father says school will spoil me for my marriage, that no man will want a woman who holds a book in her hand instead of a baby."

"Sajala, it will be years before you have babies." But she would not be comforted.

Then, one day, Sajala didn't come to class. "Dev, where is your sister today?"

"She is getting ready for her marriage."

"That's impossible! She's only fourteen! You have to get her to meet me here even if it's just for a few minutes."

The next day, Dev came with a note for me in Sajala's neat writing. "I will be there at five."

I was early, and I thought every ruffle of a leaf was Sajala. It was nearly six when at last she came.

"I was afraid you wouldn't wait for me. Memsahib Rosalind, you have to save me. The husband they have chosen for me is old and has hairs growing out of his ears and his nose, and he spits his chew of beetle leaf on the clean floor. They call him the smelly one, for in the bazaar he has a stall that sells fish, and he and the fish are as one."

"Safia, why have your parents chosen such a man for you?"

"He is asking for no dowry, and he has money to give to my Father to pay the moneylenders."

I knew about the evil moneylenders who charged huge interest payments that increased every day. "What does your mother say?"

"She is unhappy, but if Father doesn't get a hundred *rupees*, he will be punished by the moneylenders. They will beat him and take all we have."

I had an idea. It was a desperate chance, but I couldn't allow Sajala to ruin her life.

Raman's home was in an Indian neighborhood set apart from the tiny huts and makeshift shacks of the working class. His father was a well-respected lawyer, and they lived in a two-story house with a terrace on the roof to catch the cool breezes. I had never been inside his home, and now I felt awkward knocking on the door. What would his parents think of me for being so bold? An Indian girl would never compromise herself in such a way. The servant who opened the door was surprised but polite. "Come in, Memsahib, and I will summon Sahib Raman."

He showed me into the sitting room and left me to look about. The windows were shaded with mats. There was only the necessary furniture, but the walls were hung with rugs in glowing reds and blues. They looked like handfuls of blossoms had been thrown across them to make a pattern.

Raman saw me admiring them. "Those are Persian rugs, some of them as much as five hundred years old. My father collects them. As a boy I wondered why they were on the walls instead of the floor where I could walk over them barefooted to feel their softness, but Father explained they were made of silk and not meant for walking on."

"You must wonder why I've come storming into your home."

"I'm delighted to have you as a guest. What can I offer you to drink? A glass of *lassi* or some lemonade?"

"Nothing, thank you. Those rugs must be worth a great deal."

"Yes, my mother sometimes winces when Father comes home with a new one under his arm."

"What I mean is, your family could afford to give money to someone who wanted to marry you."

"Rosalind, this is so sudden. How much do you think you are worth? I would say a great deal, certainly more than a Persian rug."

"No, you idiot. I'm not talking about myself."

"Ah, what a disappointment. I envisioned long evenings alone with you discussing politics and working out schemes to gain Indian independence. Perhaps you would teach me to spin?"

"Raman, this is serious. I want you to marry Sajala."

"Of course, my pleasure. Anything for you. Now who is this woman who is to be my bride?"

"I've told you about Sajala. She's the girl who comes to my school for boys, and she is very bright and very pretty."

"Ah, better and better. And how old is this prize student of yours?"

"She's fourteen, and her family are making her marry this old man with hair in his ears and nose, because they need to pay off moneylenders."

"And you think I should go to my father and say, 'Father, could you sell a few of your beloved rugs so that I can marry this child whom I have never seen, but whose father is in debt to moneylenders?'"

"You won't do it?"

"Rosalind, let's be serious. Just think what you are asking of me. You want me to marry someone I don't know or love. That may be the old way, but I'm not like that. If I'm going to spend the rest of my life with someone, it must be someone I care for and someone I have something in common with. The last thing I would consider doing is buying a bride. Our magazine has written endless articles trying to abolish the evils of selling off a girl against her will."

"But it won't be against her will. She'll like you much more than the old man who smells of fish."

"That's faint praise indeed. I'm sorry to disappoint you, but the answer is no. Now let me at least get you some refreshments for your trouble."

But I was already on my way out. I saw how stupid I had been. I wondered if Raman would ever forgive my foolishness. I was desperate. I had a few shillings of my own, but not nearly enough to pay Sajala's father's debts.

No one in the family knew about my school except Aunt Louise. I found her in her room, just changing out of the nurse's uniform she wore at the orphanage. "I'm absolutely the most stupid person in the world," I told her.

"That usually means you have acted without thinking, Rosy. Better confess."

I told her the whole miserable story of begging Raman to marry Sajala. "I couldn't just let her marry that man she hates."

"I can certainly see why Raman might be just the least put out. After all, weren't you asking him to do exactly what Sajala's parents were asking her to do: to marry against his wishes someone he hardly knew?"

"I suppose when you put it like that. But what can I do?"

"Tell me a little of this girl, Sajala."

"She flies through her tasks at home so she can sit for an hour in our class. She's so quick to learn, and it doesn't bother her to have to learn with boys much younger than she is. She's quiet, but she's always listening."

"Rosy, can you bring Sajala to our house?"

Sajala was shy about accompanying me, looking about our home in wonderment and keeping close to me. Aunt Louise coaxed her into a chair, but Sajala sat on its very edge, ready to flee at the least thing.

In a firm voice, Aunt Louise said to her, "Instead of marrying this gentleman, Sajala, would you prefer living here with us? We would give you an opportunity to learn reading and writing, and at the orphanage, nursing."

Sajala looked from Aunt Louise to me and back again, waiting for one of us to take back the offer. When she saw Aunt Louise meant what she said, Sajala jumped out of the chair. "Yes, yes, please!"

The next day, Sajala and Dev led Aunt Louise and me to the miserable hut where her parents lived. Her father, who repaired shoes for a living, was seated outside, scraping away on a bit of leather with a curved knife. He was a short, compact man who appeared packed with energy. His hair stood up on his head in an alert way, and his eyes were wide open. When Mr. Camul saw the four of us approaching, he jumped up, spilling his work. "Oh, Dev, my son, what evil thing have you done?"

Mrs. Camul hurried out to see what was happening. "Dev, have you given your teacher trouble? Sajala, why aren't you at the river scrubbing the clothes?" She threw the end of her *sari* over her head, as if she couldn't bear to see what was coming next.

"Dev is in no trouble. He's one of my best pupils." I didn't mention that he'd put a toad in my book bag. Sajala looked too frightened to answer her mother.

Aunt Louise made a very proper *namaste*. "I am Louise Hartley, the aunt of your son's teacher. I apologize for disturbing you. I have something I would like to say to the two of you, that is, if you have a moment."

Mr. Camul looked confused, but he managed, "Yes, certainly, Memsahib, we have as many moments as you wish."

"Perhaps you didn't know, but Sajala has been going to school with Dev."

Sajala's mother said, "What have I done to have such an unfortunate child? So that is what you do when you disappear in the afternoons, telling me the shopping took long because you had to argue the price everywhere?"

Sajala squeezed behind the trunk of a neem tree, trying to make herself invisible. "Yes, hide yourself," her father said. "What if your future husband learns you are making such a fool of yourself? He will have nothing to do with a wife who does not know her place."

"That is just what I have come to speak about," Aunt Louise said. "The man who has made you an offer for Sajala may not wish her to read and write, but I have been looking for someone with just such qualities."

Mr. Camul asked, "What good to you is a servant who will not do a proper job of cleaning because she has always a pencil in her hand?"

"I have no need of a servant to clean for me. I want someone to help us at the orphanage and someone to write my letters and to read to me. I find my eyes tire easily."

The last part was a lie. If Aunt Louise had a book in her hand she liked, she would sit for hours, and if she were reading out of doors and it rained, you had to drag her into the house.

"We have found her a husband," Mr. Camul said. "There can be no question of her slaving with a pencil."

"How much has this man offered for her?" Aunt Louise asked.

When he told her, Aunt Louise said, "I will give you again as much. She must live with us until she is twenty-one, but you may come and see her as often as you like."

Sajala left the neem tree and threw herself at her father's feet. "Please, Papa, let me go with the Memsahib Hartley and the Memsahib James. Please, please, don't make me marry the old man."

Sajala's mother came out from behind her *sari*. "When she is twenty-one, you would throw her out in the cold. The old one would not do that."

"You misunderstand me, Mrs. Camul. When Sajala is twenty-one, she can do as she likes."

Mrs. Camul looked bewildered. "Who can do as they like? What nonsense is that?"

"I mean that when she is twenty-one, she might want to get married or, if she wished, she could stay on with us. Perhaps she will learn to be a nurse at the orphanage."

Sajala's father had a crafty look. "If she should find a husband even at such an old age, would you pay her dowry price?"

"If her husband asks for a dowry, I would give it."

"Then you can take her."

Then there was a lot of drama. Sajala laughed and cried and commenced chewing on the end of her braid in her happiness. Her mother ran to her and embraced her, Dev looked like he had arranged the whole thing himself, and Mr. Camul stood apart, appearing pleased at the deal he had made. Finally, he smiled upon his daughter, who had made that good deal possible.

Before making her offer, Aunt Louise had discussed her plan with Mother and Father, who were skeptical but agreed. In spite of Aunt Louise's plan, however, they looked at Sajala as a sort of lady's maid like Amina. When Aunt Ethyl began to order Sajala about, though, Aunt Louise put a stop to it. "Sajala must have time for her lessons and time to learn nursing at the orphanage. If you need to have someone to order about, you must find such a person, but it will not be Sajala."

For her part, Sajala moved through our home like a shadow, trying to make herself inconspicuous. She confided

177

to me, "Rosalind,"—for I wouldn't let her call me Mem-sahib anymore—"I am in heaven. I know that not every-one is like your good Aunt Louise or Mrs. Nelson at the orphanage. Here your family sees me as a poor Indian girl in their midst, and so I am, but I will study and keep myself neat and do as I am told. And if I have any unhappiness, I will think of myself locked in the home of the old man and the unhappiness will go away."

Aunt Louise confided to me, "Rosy, I am freeing India one person at a time."

Seeing my aunt's delight in Sajala's progress, watching her pick out new *saris* and a nursing uniform for Sajala, and hearing her read bits from her favorite books to Sajala, I was sure it was less a gesture of freeing Sajala than one of binding her up with love, love for the daughter Aunt Louise might have had. For Aunt Louise had once been in love. Aunt Ethyl had sent her sister's fiance away, keeping Aunt Louise from marrying. But no one spoke of that anymore.

16

Sajala became part of our daily lives. Little by little her gentle ways and her constant curiosity began to endear her to the whole family. Even Aunt Ethyl took to her willingness to learn and to be useful.

I was secretly following Dickie and David's travels in India. They journeyed to another colony of England, Burma, visiting cities with lovely names like Rangoon and Mandalay. In the middle of January they were back in India, in Madras, where there was violence. The owner of a cinema decorated his theater with patriotic British flags in honor of the Prince of Wales's visit, and this enraged some anti-British Indians. They tried to destroy the cinema, and the owner shot one of them. This set me to wondering what all my dreams for India's freedom might lead to. Like me, Max was devastated. "Violence is just what we don't want. It's what Gandhi has spent his life opposing." He wrote an angry editorial in *Young India* against violence, and Gandhi talked of another fast.

I read that Dickie and David were with the *maharaja* of Mysore, out catching wild elephants. I was sure they had long since forgotten their afternoon with me in Calcutta.

In our family the news of His Royal Highness was not the most important news. Colonel Brighten had come calling on Aunt Louise. In the ship that brought Aunt Louise and me from England to India two years earlier, the colonel sat next to her in the dining room every night for three weeks. He taught her how to crack the claws of lobsters and took her to shipboard dances. They became good friends and at the end of the voyage, exchanged addresses. He returned to Oxford University where he was the headmaster of Balliol College and now here he was.

Aunt Louise could not stop blushing, while Aunt Ethyl accused her of acting like a sixteen-year old. "Have you no dignity, Louise?" she said, and when that did not make

Aunt Louise send away Colonel Brighten, Aunt Ethyl raised questions about the colonel's background. "I am very suspicious of a man who appears out of nowhere seeking the acquaintance of a wealthy woman. Who knows what he is after."

Father put an end to that speculation. "There is no question about the man's background. I know all about him. He led a brigade nearby me in Mesopotamia. An excellent fellow, and now he's here in India preparing a report on Indian universities for the British government."

Aunt Ethyl quickly said, "Then he will soon be returning to England."

"Oh, yes. He is a headmaster at Balliol College at Oxford. As to money, he has his own."

When the colonel asked Aunt Louise to marry him, the whole house was turned upside down. Aunt Ethyl complained of horrible headaches and took all her meals in her room. Father thought the position, as the wife of the headmaster of Balliol College, could not be improved upon and encouraged the marriage. Mother could not bear the idea of losing her favorite sister and took to her chaise longue. I was happy for Aunt Louise and encouraged her, but it was hard to imagine our little family without her ability to turn

181

the cold words of Aunt Ethyl into something more human.

The colonel came every day with flowers to persuade Aunt Louise. I heard them chatting away in the garden. The colonel said, "My dear Louise, I know how fond you are of India—I am enchanted with this country myself—but you're British. Everyone at the university will adore you as I do."

"It's so cold in England, Arbuthnot. My toes were never warm."

"But here in India you swelter half the year, and then you are drowned in the monsoon rains the rest of the year. Besides, I would not allow your toes to be cold."

"Arbuthnot, there is a more serious problem. I am afraid we differ on our beliefs about India."

"You know I respect your thoughts on the subject of India's independence, and I hope you respect mine on the importance of Britain's role in India."

"Yes, of course, but how could I leave Sajala? I have accepted responsibility for her."

"Then she must come with us. We would all make her welcome."

"It would be too strange for her."

Father and Mother promised to take care of Sajala.

Mrs. Nelson said she would continue Sajala's nurse's training. Aunt Louise was not convinced. "Rosy," she said to me, "when I am gone, Ethyl will order Sajala about, and I won't be here to protect her. And I will miss all the children at the orphanage. I like to think some of my special pets there would miss me."

In the end, India won out. "I care a great deal for Arbuthnot," Aunt Louise confessed to me. We were in the garden room, the windows open to the evening breezes. Outside, an enormous moon cast the stripes of tree shadows across the lawn. A stork drifted down and, folding its great wings, settled on the top of a mango tree. "I'm afraid I care more for India. It's where I gained my freedom and now, in the hour of India's need, I can't leave the Indian people to fight alone for their freedom. Arbuthnot would not agree with me on my hopes; it would be something separating us."

Aunt Louise licked away a tear that had made its way down her cheek. At least this time when an admirer went away it was Aunt Louise's choice. Colonel Arbuthnot Brighten, vice chancellor of Oxford, returned to England, Mother left her chaise longue, and Aunt Ethyl recovered from her headaches. The colonel, with his talk of England, had made Father homesick, and now he began to talk of how his leave was due and to speculate on taking us with him to England for a few months. But nothing came of his talk, for Father could not imagine anyone else doing his job, even for a few months.

Sajala was upset. "I can see the colonel Sahib was not like the man I was ordered to marry. There are no hairs sticking out from his ears and nose, and he smells as pleasant as a sandalwood tree. I think if it were not for me, Memsahib would marry the nice man. I heard Memsahib Ethyl say that for once she was happy I was in this house because if it were not so, her sister would surely have gone away to England with the colonel."

I tried to reassure her. "No, Sajala, you mustn't think that way. Aunt Louise loves India. That's why she is staying here. She couldn't bear to leave this country."

Sajala wasn't convinced. Her heart was no longer in her lessons. She had progressed to long division, but now she asked, "What good does it do me how many times one long number fits into another long number? When in my life will I ever see such long numbers?" At the orphanage her tears fell upon the puzzled children, who did not know what they had done to make their young nurse so unhappy. Finally, Mrs. Nelson had to speak to Sajala. "You must cheer up. You are making the children worry."

"You see," Sajala said to me, "I am good for nothing, Rosalind. I am making everyone unhappy," and she would not be cheered. The next day she was gone.

Aunt Louise and I went at once to her home to see if she was there. Her father was indignant. "This is very bad. I give you my daughter, and now you lose her."

Her mother accused, "She is a good girl and would only run away if you were cruel to her."

"Mrs. Camul, Sajala was happy with us," Aunt Louise said. "She didn't run away because we mistreated her but because she believed she was keeping me from doing something I wished to do."

If Sajala wasn't at her home, where could she be? That evening, we were all together in the dining room. It was suppertime, but no one was eating. "I am certainly to blame," Aunt Louise said. "I only meant to rescue her from enslavement to that old man, and see what I have done. I can't bear to think of her alone and helpless in some city. I hope, Ethyl, that you said nothing unkind to her that would have made her want to leave."

"Louise, that is uncalled for. You know I thought the

whole thing a foolish notion from the beginning, but I can assure you I would not be so cruel as to tell her that."

"Yes, yes, I apologize for accusing you. I am just so upset. Harlan, isn't there something the government can do? Can't we have the police out looking for her?"

"Louise, you must be sensible. There are thousands of Indians missing for one reason or another. We can't send the police out to investigate everyone who lies dead on the streets."

Aunt Louise let out a little cry. For once, Mother was angry with Father. Instead of retreating to her chaise longue, she said, "Harlan, just think how that sounds. How can you be so cruel?"

Gopel came in from the kitchen, tying on his apron, for unless he knew Mother would see him, he refused to wear an apron, saying it got in the way of his cooking. And that was true, for Gopel went at food like he was wrestling a crocodile. Now he said, "No plates have come back to me." He looked at the untouched food. "Something is wrong? I put poison in the food? I got that fish fresh. If it is not a good fish, I will stuff it down the throat of the fisherman who sold it to me."

"No, Gopel," Mother said. "There is nothing wrong

with the fish. We have just been talking among ourselves."

"This room is for eating," Gopel said. "Now you have a cold fish," he scolded. Untying his apron, he returned to the kitchen, where we knew he would sulk and for revenge serve us weak tea and stale biscuits for dessert.

Ranjit hurried into the room. "Now what?" Father said. "I hope there is no trouble, Ranjit."

"Sahib James. An Indian man unknown to me is at the door with Sajala. Is that trouble?"

We were all at the door. An elderly man stood there with a firm grip on Sajala's arm. He made a very proper *namaste* and introduced himself. "I am Ajay Bahadur." Ignoring us women, who were crowding around Sajala, he said to Father, "This girl came to me and said she wanted to be my wife, but her mother and father had told me you bought her for a wife." He was staring right at Father.

Father turned red and got all indignant. "You completely misunderstand, sir. My sister-in-law is training her to be a nurse. There was never any question of her being my wife. I have a wife."

Mother smiled brightly at the man to indicate that, indeed, she was the proper wife.

Aunt Louise had her arm around Sajala. "Why ever did

187

you run away? We were so worried and miserable when we couldn't find you."

Mr. Bahadur was saying, "I won't be accused of taking what is not mine. You bought her, now you must have her. What is more, if she ran away, she must have done something bad. Why should I want such a wife to make me miserable in my old age?"

It was true he was old and he had hair growing out of his ears and his nose, but he was a proper gentleman, doing what was right and not keeping Sajala when she offered to be his wife. Father was impressed as well. "Mr. Bahadur, we are very grateful to you for returning Sajala. Give us a chance to reward your kindness. Will you stop to take tea with us?"

Mr. Bahadur sat down at the table with great dignity, looking closely at our plates. "May I ask where you get your fish? Those are not my fish. They are soft fleshed and pale. See how clouded the eyes are. You must come to my fish stall. You will see how bright the eyes of my fish are, as if they had come just that moment from the sea." Then, while a puzzled Gopel brought in tea for Mr. Bahadur and Sajala clung to Aunt Louise, our guest gave a long talk on the superiority of his fish and how they were caught in the deepest, freshest water. "Not where the lazy fishermen cast their nets and all the refuse of the city lies close by. No, my men are not afraid to venture out in the river."

When he had finished his tea, he again made his *namaste* and, thanking us, left us in a most dignified way.

Father said, "The man is much too old for you, Sajala, but he is a gentleman and obviously a good businessman. He would have provided very well for you."

"Harlan!" Aunt Louise was incensed. "Sajala is not to be sold to the best provider. Sajala, if you could have seen how worried we were, you would have been convinced we all wanted you here with us, and now you must promise you will never run away again."

Meekly, Sajala promised, and the cold fish was removed and the weak tea and stale biscuits served by a vengeful Gopel, who had overhead the criticism of his fish.

17

The next day a package arrived addressed to me. It didn't come in the post but by special messenger, and its wrappings were impressive. Oddly, there was no return address. A package by special messenger was not an everyday occurrence, and my entire family was looking over my shoulder as I opened it. The box had Harrods' name on it. Harrods was one of the most elegant of the department stores in London. I cautiously removed the cover, and there, affixed to a delicate lace veil, were three perfectly curled ostrich feathers and an invitation to be presented to King George and Queen Mary. There was no card, but none was needed, for no one but a member of the royal family would issue such an invitation. My heart was pounding. Though he was still on his journey, it could only have come from David. It was unbelievable, but he must have gone to the trouble of having it sent to me.

I had made fun of young women presented at court. I had laughed at all the fuss, but it didn't take long for a very small part of me to see myself going through the doors of Buckingham Palace, ostrich feathers flying, and curtsying to the king and queen, who would want to know who that charming girl was. The vision of myself in court was so amazing I could hardly believe it, and yet it was all I could think about.

Everyone set about trying to guess who was responsible for the invitation. "It must have come from that nice Lord Louis," Aunt Louise said, but Father knew royal procedure. "I think not," he said, and gave me a questioning look. But soon, excitement overcame speculation.

"You must certainly go," Aunt Ethyl said. "You could not possibly refuse so important an invitation. And with our empty house on Lord North Street, we would not have the worry or expense of a hotel."

"You know I have been talking of taking a leave," Father said. "I do finally believe young Beasley is up to handling the office—for a very short time, of course."

Aunt Louise, who had guessed it was the prince, was thinking romantic thoughts. "Oh, Rosy, just imagine, that dear boy remembered you." She stroked the arrangement of feathers as if it were an exotic pet.

"We must give some serious thought to what you will wear," Mother said. "White, of course—that's traditional—and a train. You must have elbow-length white gloves in the softest kid. We can shop for them in Harrods once we get to London."

It was all happening too fast. "You're all just assuming that I'll put feathers in my hair and curtsy to the king. What if I don't want to go?"

They looked at me as though I had lost my reason. "My dear girl," Father said, "no one can force you to be presented to the king, but there are thousands of young women who would give anything to be in your shoes."

Aunt Ethel was quick to add, "I hope you are aware of the enormous honor that has been bestowed on you. You will have a story to pass on to your children and grandchildren."

Mother was still thinking about clothes. "Of course you must go, and your aunts and I will need gowns. Harlan, I suppose you would wear your uniform? How fortunate you have just had Baneet alter it."

It was Aunt Louise who understood my hesitation. "You must do as you please, Rosy, but remember our purpose is not to do away with the British Empire but to allow India to build its own empire."

I did not think Gandhi wanted to sit on a throne and have young Indian girls in ostrich feathers and long white gowns curtsying to him, but I kept silent, for I could not say that with Father and Aunt Ethyl there.

My silence was taken for acceptance, and everyone hurried off to make preparations. When later I saw a letter from Aunt Louise to Colonel Brighten laying with the outgoing mail for one of the *chota malis* to carry to the post office, I decided turning down David's offer would make too many people unhappy. What I refused to admit to myself was that I was pleased to have an excuse to go. Alone in my room I had tried on the ostrich feathers and convinced myself that I looked regal, not foolish.

Max saw only the foolish part. "What? You are going to stick feathers in your head and grovel to the king and queen?"

"In my hair, and not grovel, just curtsy. Anyhow,

getting to know the prince was your idea."

I was not the only one returning to England. Raman's father insisted that Raman become a solicitor as he was. He had made arrangements for Raman to become a barrister; that is, he would be arguing law in the courts. "My father thinks working through the court is a faster way for India's independence than my writing articles in a magazine the British don't read. I'm not convinced he's right, but Gandhi started out as a barrister. Father has found a firm of barristers who will take me in. They're members of the Inner Temple, one of four Inns of Court. You have to be a member of one of the Inns to practice law in England. I'll be apprenticed for a year before I can practice."

Max was jealous. "It's not fair for the two of you to traipse off to England and leave me here. There's so much the three of us could do in England as a team. We could make speeches at Hyde Park and get up some demonstrations."

"Max, you know there is nothing more important to me than India's freedom. Look at the chance I took in getting the letter to the prince. I've done everything I can think of doing and got myself in every kind of trouble to do it. But this is different," I cautioned him. "That's not what I'm going to England for. I'm supposed to be a model daughter of the empire, making homage to the king, not an Indian revolutionary on a mission to destroy the empire. That doesn't change how I feel. It's just that however much I may want to, I can't give a speech for India's freedom in Buckingham Palace."

Max was giving me an intense look. "Buckingham Palace. Of course. I hadn't thought it out. If you could get Gandhi's letter into the hands of the prince, how much better if you could get Gandhi's message to the king."

"Don't be ridiculous. I'll be just one of dozens of girls who are presented, and I won't be anywhere near the king."

Raman said, "Did you think Rosy would drop a letter from Gandhi as she backed out of the throne room and the king would dash over and pick it up? You must be out of your head, Max."

But Max always had a way of firing my desire for India's freedom. Suddenly, I had a vision of myself in a London jail, my white kid gloves rusty from clinging to the bars, my train dragging, and my ostrich feathers drooping. But I would be in England, and something I did would have put me in that prison, something important. I could hardly wait.

. . .

No one is more organized than Father. In no time he had booked passage for us on a ship sailing later this month of April. At his office, Father prepared Beasley, who was looking thin and pale under the ordeal, and Mother and my aunts put Baneet to work and began the packing of so many trunks I was afraid the ship would sink.

Raman had already sailed, and Sajala was staying at the Nelsons'. Knowing she would see Max every day, I was a little jealous, but Max was seldom home. In March, Gandhi had been arrested in the city of Ahmadabad and taken by a secret train to Fort Bombay jail. He was charged with "promoting disaffection against the Government through his writings." Even in this he would not quarrel, and amazingly, pleaded guilty!

When I asked Max why Gandhi would do such a thing, he said, "Gandhi is determined there will be no violent demonstrations against his arrest. Besides, he says it is exactly what he has been doing and will continue to do."

"Max, I hate the idea of going to the very country that's responsible for imprisoning Gandhi."

"That's exactly where you should be going. They need people who can tell them the truth about India."

"You think I'll go about to teas and balls carrying a sign supporting Gandhi's campaign for India's freedom from the very people who supply me with cucumber sandwiches and dancing partners?"

"Perhaps not a sign, but I expect you to whisper the need for Indian's freedom in the ears of your dancing partners and to step on their toes if they don't agree."

18

I had doubts and forebodings until the very day the ship pulled out of Bombay. Whatever Max said, I couldn't help feeling that boarding a ship that would take me to England was treason on my part. Aunt Louise and I stood together at the ship's rail, the only two in our little group who were thinking of what we were leaving and not what we were sailing toward.

"Rosy," Aunt Louise said, "the only thing that allows me to leave India is the certain knowledge that I will return."

Whatever our doubts, we were soon caught up in what was happening on board. The very first day out, Aunt Louise saved the life of a little boy.

"I was sitting in one of the deck chairs having a nice cup of tea, Darjeeling with two sugars," Aunt Louise told us later, "and thinking of nothing particular, when a little fellow who couldn't have been more than five or six years old raced past me and clambered up on the railing, leaning over to call to someone on the deck below. He leaned so far out that had I not rushed to grab him by the shirt collar, he was sure to have fallen. Right behind me was a delightful young girl, about your age, Rosy, who was also racing to save the child. She introduced herself as Jane Garves. The child, Timothy, was her brother. Then nothing would do, but I must meet the whole family—her father, Brigadier General Garves, her mother, and a great number of children of assorted ages. It appears there is also an older son who is up at Oxford and wasn't with them. They have been visiting India with their father, who had some business with the viceroy, and the family is now returning to their home in London. They appear to be one of England's first families."

At dinner that evening we found ourselves sitting with the Garveses at the captain's table. "We arranged it," Mrs. Garves said. "We are so grateful to Miss Hartley for saving Timothy from tumbling over the rail to his certain death.

I don't know what we will do with that child. There is nothing he will not get up to. He is as bad as my husband."

We all looked a little startled at that, but the general only laughed. He said, "If she could have found a way, my dear Lucinda would have traveled to Mesopotamia with me during the war and forbid me to carry out orders."

At that, Father said, "Mesopotamia! I was there with my battalion of Gurkha Rifles." Then they were off a mile a minute comparing notes on battles, leaving Mrs. Garves and my mother and aunts to discuss London shops. Mother begged advice from Mrs. Garves, for we could all see from the elegance of her dress that she would be an excellent resource.

Jane, who sat next to me, leaned over and said in a low voice, "All that shop talk is a lot of rot. I'd much rather hear about India from you. We were only there for a few weeks, but I fell in love with the country and envy you for living there. You have to tell me all about it. I only wish I had known you when we were there. Do you have tigers in your yard and all that sort of thing?"

"Well, not tigers, but monkeys and bandicoots and lovely lizards and birds in every color imaginable, and trees that weep yellow blossoms and plants that smell better than

French perfume, and there's the bazaar, where you can buy paper kites or jewels."

"Oh, I knew it! I knew you were someone I could talk with. You can tell me all the things I missed. I mean to go back again and stay forever."

"Why couldn't you stay longer this time?"

"Oh, the most horrid thing imaginable. I have to be presented to the king and queen and preen about in white feathers."

"Jane! I'm going to be presented at court too. Oh, I hope we do it together. I'm sure I'm going to make an awful fool of myself."

"Oh, someone always does. It's such good fun. They trip over their train or fall over backing out or their feathers aren't properly fastened and the feathers float to the floor. A page is there specially to run over and pick them up."

"How awful!"

"We'll have to rehearse together. We'll take turns being the king and queen. Maybe we should make history and do something really outrageous. Wear a red petticoat under our white dress and pull up our skirts to show it when we curtsy."

I looked about to be sure no one was listening, but

they were all chattering away. I whispered, "I know what I'd like to do. I'd like to tell the king he must give India its freedom."

"Oh, you must meet my brother, Joey. He is absolutely mad on the subject of that little man Gandhi. He and Father kill each other every time they're together. Father wouldn't let Joey come on the trip because he was afraid he'd cause trouble with his ideas. You mustn't let Father hear you or he won't let me be friends with you."

"My father is just the same, but I actually heard Gandhi speak, and I was arrested and got sent over to England to stay with my aunts as a punishment, and then, in London, I went to hear a speech a woman gave about independence for India and right after that I had to return to India because my mother worried so about me."

"You have had such an exciting life. You must teach me all about India and then I'll come and visit you."

The brigadier general said, "Well, you two young women are getting along like a house afire. I suppose lots of talk about what you will be wearing for the London season."

"Yes, Father," Jane said. "Rosalind is going to be presented at court this season."

"Excellent. The two of you will have much to chat about on the voyage over."

Afterward, I asked Jane, "What did your father mean by the London season?"

"It's all the most awful dreariness. Families come from their estates in the country to their London homes and go to parties at one another's houses, and you dance all night with stupid boys who sweat a lot and tell you how rich they are. All the families give balls, and we are giving one, and my brother, Joey, will be there and we'll all get up a proper revolution."

After our dinner together, Jane and I were inseparable. My family was delighted. "The brigadier general is very high up in the government and filthy rich," Father said. Mother went on about Mrs. Garves's fashionable clothes, while Aunt Ethyl spoke of the Garves's place in society. Aunt Louise became a favorite of all the little Garveses, telling them tales of India and spoiling them with sweets. When the ship docked, we parted with firm handshakes on the part of Father and Brigadier General Garves and warm embraces on the part of the women. Jane and I pledged eternal friendship.

"I'll send the Rolls-Royce for you," Jane told me.

"I've never ridden in a Rolls-Royce."

"Oh, you funny girl. You have as much to learn about London as I have about India."

The first glimpse of my aunts' house on Lord North Street gave me the shivers. It was there that I had been exiled from India, and it was there that I rescued Aunt Louise from Aunt Ethyl's bullying ways and took her with me to India, not guessing that Aunt Ethyl would follow us on the next boat. Mother and Father were delighted with the house. It had been Mother's home as a child, and she wandered from room to room recalling her childhood growing up with Aunt Louise and Aunt Ethyl, but there was no question as to who was in charge of Lord North Street. Aunt Ethyl assigned everyone their rooms and set the hour for breakfast, lunch, and dinner. Rita had been called back to duty, and Aunt Ethyl met with her each morning to decide on the menu of the day, a very frugal one.

At first Aunt Louise tried to take part in these sessions, begging for a nice joint of beef and chocolate cake instead of shepherd's pie and a plain pudding. "Ethyl, that is all very well for you and for me, but Cecelia and Harlan and Rosalind are our guests, and we must do better for them."

"Louise, you must leave it to me to manage the house. You were never good at such things."

It looked like Aunt Louise was falling into her old ways and meekly surrendering. However, Father, faced with shepherd's pie and plain pudding, said rather wistfully, "I had been expecting a nice joint for my first meal back in England."

Aunt Louise sat up very straight and said, "You shall have it tomorrow evening, Harlan, and as many evenings after that as you wish."

Aunt Ethyl became very red in the face, but she knew when she was outnumbered, and Rita was soon serving platters of lamb, and mutton, and beef nice and bloody as Father liked it. Now it was Father and not Aunt Ethyl who ruled Lord North Street.

19

Father delighted in the location of the house. Lord North Street was only a few blocks from the Houses of Parliament. Any evening, you would see doors open in the neighboring homes as members of the House of Commons made their way to cast an evening vote. One night, Father followed the members to the House of Commons to sit in the Strangers' Gallery, where anyone might observe parliamentary business.

At breakfast the next morning, Father said, "The prime minister made an excellent speech on India last night. Lloyd George has it just right. He said there was much to cause grave concern about rebels wanting freedom for

India, but nothing to fear. Gandhi is in jail, and that's an end to the whole business of giving India over to a bunch of upstarts."

I couldn't be still. "Not just upstarts, Father. Gandhi may be in prison, but he has thousands and thousands of loyal followers."

"Rosalind, you disappoint me. I had thought now that you were back in England you would have developed some loyalty to your king and country. Instead I find you are still concerned with that treasonous little man."

"Harlan, Rosy, dear," Mother said, "let's not waste this wonderful time in London on disagreements." Father and I were both sorry for Mother, who looked like she would retreat to the Lord North Street equivalent of her chaise longue.

I apologized, and Father grunted in a conciliatory sort of way.

Mother had been looking forward to our visit that day to Harrod's. But we were disappointed by the elegant department store. The women who waited on us were haughty and superior, making us feel like the exiles we were. I missed the bazaars, where you simply went up to a merchant and began to bargain and, after settling on a price, shook hands and were friends.

When Mother chose a dress for me, the saleslady said, "Madame, are you quite convinced of your choice? I would suggest this frock, so much more suitable for the young lady."

Mother glanced at the price and frowned, whereupon the woman bristled. "Of course, if it is the price that will determine the frock, we can look again." By the end of the day we were so unsettled, nothing had been purchased. All that changed when Mrs. Garves and Jane swept us up in their Rolls-Royce the next morning and took us shopping. The same saleslady who had been so cold to us changed entirely, "Oh, Mrs. Garves, I had no idea Mrs. James was a friend of yours. I am sure we can find something suitable."

"I should hope so," Mrs. Garves said, "and don't try to foist your extravagant frocks on us. You know I consider them vulgar. This young woman will shine in a simple dress."

Out came dress after dress, silks and taffetas and the finest muslins and linens. Where were all these dresses the day before? Mrs. Garves and Jane gave us hints and listened carefully to Mother's opinion, which they pronounced "elegant." Leaving the abashed and defeated saleswoman to send the dresses we chose to Lord North Street. Mrs. Garves and Jane then took us to their home on Hyde Park for tea. As we made our way through the London streets in the luxurious car I thought if one had an automobile the size of the Rolls-Royce, one would hardly need a home.

Their butler, Edgar, opened the door to us, and we swept up a grand stairway to a tasteful sitting room that was all cozy chairs and sofas with tall windows that looked out onto the park. I couldn't help thinking of Aunt Louise and myself on my first visit to London and meeting Max in the park, where he was making an impassioned speech to passersby on freedom for India. Aunt Louise must have been thinking of the same thing, for when I looked at her, she gave me a quick secret smile.

Tea was poured from a silver service by Edgar, and scones and little cucumber sandwiches were handed round by a maid in black with a frilly white apron and cap. Later, when we had left the formal tea and escaped to her room, I told Jane all about Max's speech. "What a pity your friend isn't here," she said. "I should love to meet him."

"I have another friend, Raman, who *is* here. He's Indian, and he's going to be a lawyer. He's very handsome."

Jane stared at me. "You're not in love with him, are you? You went all red when you mentioned his name. I want him for myself. He sounds so much better than all the foolish boys around here. I'll tell you what. You can have my brother, and I'll have your Raman."

I laughed, trying not to take Jane seriously, but I wasn't at all sure about the bargain. Joey probably was very nice, but he couldn't be as nice as Raman.

The next day I had a chance to judge Joey for myself, for he was down from Oxford to attend the ball the Garveses were giving the following evening for Jane. It wasn't the Rolls-Royce this time that picked me up but a small, roofless car Jane called a roadster. Joey sprang out of the driver's seat to open the door for me. He was stretched out and quite thin. He bristled with energy, and even his sandy hair stood up as if electricity were running all through him. He had the grin of a friendly dog, and words spilled out of him one on top of the other.

"You are Rosalind, and you and I and your Indian friend and my idiot sister are going to free India among the four of us. Now where will we find your Raman?"

I hardly knew what to say. Joey was moving so quickly. He was pulling my world right into his. Breathless, I

210

managed to say, "Raman is apprenticed, articled I think you call it, to some lawyers at the Inner Temple." With misgivings I handed him the name of the lawyers. There were several all connected like so many links on a chain: Severville, Nestled, Garrot, Spindid, Raykel, and Burble. "I don't think he'll be able to get away in the middle of the day." I hoped by some magic he would, for I hadn't seen or talked with Raman, and I longed to know how he was getting on.

"Oh, no problem at all," Joey said, pushing down so hard on the gas pedal I had to hang on to keep from flying out of the little car. "Burble handles Father's business. He's terribly intimidated by Father. I'll just suggest Father might want to see Raman. That's not exactly a lie, you understand, for Father might want to see Raman or he might not. None of Burble's business. We're all going to the Strangers' Gallery because someone is raising a question in the Commons about Gandhi's imprisonment."

Here was something I knew. "Oh, I can tell you all about his imprisonment," I said. "I've had letters from Max, who knows a guard inside the jail. Gandhi is allowed his special diet of goats' milk, bread, oranges, lemons, and raisins. At first they weren't going to give him the food he asked for, but they agreed on 'medical grounds.' They won't let him have books or newspapers, though."

"Rosalind, you are a treasure of information." Joey was so delighted to hear what I had to say that, I noticed, his hair became even more lively.

He left Jane and me in the roadster while he rushed up the stairway of the offices of Raman's law firm. "I told you he was a dear," Jane said. "And I can tell he already adores you."

Moments later he appeared with Raman. Jane turned quickly to me. "He is gorgeous, and I must have him." She hopped out of the front seat and told me to sit there next to Joey, and she got in my place in the back and motioned Raman to sit next to her.

It was satisfying to have Raman first take my hand and ask how I was and show how happy he was to see me. "Your friend has kidnapped me," he said. "Mr. Burble was so impressed with my having an acquaintance who was the son of the Garveses he told me to take the day off."

Reluctantly, I introduced him to Jane. At once she said, "You are to sit next to me and tell me everything about yourself, starting with your very first step and your first word."

"Do shut up, Jane," Joey said, "Raman will think you even a greater fool than you are. Pay her no attention, my dear fellow. We have serious business ahead of us. They are discussing the imprisonment of Gandhi this afternoon, and your friend Rosalind seems to know all about it."

"I'm sure she has had letters on the subject from our mutual friend, Max Nelson. I've had the same information. It's an outrage. Gandhi is not even allowed pen and paper, so it's impossible for him to communicate. We wouldn't know any of this except for Max's knowing one of the prison guards."

Joey ran the car up onto the sidewalk to avoid a traffic tie-up, then back down into the street. At the Houses of Parliament it looked as if there were no parking spaces, but with a bit of bumping two cars about, Joey was able to squeeze into a spot. He jumped out of the roadster and ushered us into Parliament as though he were walking into a neighborhood grocery shop. I was terrified that we would be stopped, but a guard standing at the stairway that led to the Strangers' Gallery gave us no more than a quick look, probably thinking we were amusing ourselves between sorties into expensive stores and restaurants.

The gallery looked down on the House of Commons

and its rows of members seated on green leather benches. The speaker, regal in his robes and wig, sat at the end of the room on a platform. I couldn't help being impressed and I was sure Raman was as well, for we exchanged pleased looks. We were seeing an institution we had read about and one that had existed for centuries. However unfair I thought it. Joey immediately put us to rights.

"Bunch of silly old men with their heads buried in the sand. We'll soon show them a little excitement. I've got a nice surprise for them."

We settled onto the gallery's front row of seats. As we leaned over the edge a member of the Commons rose. He received a nod from the speaker to go ahead with what he had to say. "I would suggest to my esteemed colleagues that there are altogether too many positions in the Indian Civil Service handed over to the Indian people. At this rate the rule of India will soon have passed out of England's hands."

I jumped at the sound of a shout next to me. "And a good thing, too!" It was Joey. All the heads of the members swiveled to look up in our direction. A guard marched over to Joey and said, "We must have order, or you will be removed." My face was burning, but Raman looked rather pleased.

Another member rose and, after a friendly glance at us, addressed the Commons. "It would seem I am not alone in my belief that it is high time the responsibility for governing India be awarded to the citizens of that country. Even now, as we speak, one of India's statesmen, Mahatma Gandhi, is languishing in prison with a sentence of ten years for no greater crime then desiring that the people of India be allowed to rule their own country. Surely that is an injustice."

In spite of the warning of the guard, the four of us cheered mightily. The next thing I knew, Joey was standing up and waving the red and green flag of India's Congress Party. Shouts went up in the House of Commons, and guards rushed us out of the gallery, down the stairway, and into a police van. Moments later we were ushered unceremoniously into cells.

When the cell door slammed and I looked about at the wooden bench that served as a bed, the narrow window set so high I could not look out of it, the barbaric sanitary arrangements, I was furious with Joey. All I could think of was what Father would say if he found out. Yet the more I thought about it, the more I went over to Joey's side. Wasn't it time that someone stood up and told the truth?

As the morning passed I wondered if I would have to spend the next month in jail instead of putting on feathers and meeting the king. Regrets for our actions began piling up. I was sure that even Aunt Louise would have questions about Joey's stunt.

It felt like days, but it was probably no more than an hour or two when I was taken from my cell and led up a narrow passageway to a court, where I joined Joey, Raman, and Jane, who grabbed my hand and said, "Have you ever been so thrilled in your life? I can't wait to tell all my friends I have been in jail! They will be so envious."

Joey was smiling. "I'll never forget the looks on the faces of those fools when they saw the India's Congress Party flag. It might have been the devil itself. I've never enjoyed anything more."

I saw the expression on Raman's face. By contrast, for Raman this was very serious. I began to doubt Jane and Joey's commitment. It seemed what they were interested in was not so much India's freedom as an adventure they could boast and even laugh about at parties. For Raman it was his country they were amusing themselves with; the demonstration, however well meant, was no more to them than a kind of lark. Now that the excitement was over and

I saw what the results of our actions might be, I thought of Max. For all of his enthusiasm he would never have tried so foolish a stunt. It had gotten us nowhere, and it would infuriate our parents. I wished Max were with us.

The judge's solemn demeanor was sobering. He glared at us as our names were read out. At once he addressed Joey and Jane. "The two of you come from one of this country's first families. I can only guess at what your father would say to you, and I leave you to meditate on what his reaction and disappointment would be should he learn of your escapade. He turned to me. "As for you, young lady, I do hope you remember that although you make your home in India, you are a British citizen and must respect its institutions.

"It is you, Raman Mehra, that I am going to address. I am sure you are not aware of it, but your father and I were articled to the same firm of lawyers. We trained together, we ate and we drank together. We made the same mistakes and enjoyed the same little successes. I regret that I did not keep in touch with him after he returned to India, but whatever his feelings about India's independence, since he has sent you to England to take up the law I believe he would depend upon the law and not demonstrations to achieve independence. Now, I will dismiss any charges and send the four of you forth, but I hope this little interlude will cool a bit of your ardor"—and here he allowed himself the ghost of a smile—"but I trust it will not diminish your ideals."

We were a silent foursome as we climbed into the roadster. Raman insisted on sitting in the back with me, and suffering Jane's jealous looks, I let him hold my hand all the way to the Inner Temple, where we let him out.

Stopping in front of Lord North Street, Joey jumped out and opened the door of the roadster for me. "I hope you're not too disgusted with me," he said. "I was a very naughty boy."

I didn't think he looked at all sorry. We pledged to keep the whole story silent, and the next morning, when Father read out an article in the newspaper on a demonstration in Parliament, he said, "It's outrageous to allow idiots to carry out their tricks right in the Strangers' Gallery. I'm pleased to see the hooligans were carried off by the police."

Aunt Louise did look my way, but I said nothing, only keeping my eyes on my plate as if nothing in the world were more interesting than oatmeal porridge.

20

That evening, as our rented car drove up to the entrance of the Garveses' home for the ball, we were only one of a hundred automobiles and certainly one of the most humble, but however modest our car, we were all in our very best outfits, with Father's medals marching across his uniform, Aunt Ethyl sedate in black silk, Mother swathed in delicate lace, and Aunt Louise glowing in blue satin, for she had learned from Colonel Brighten that he was to be at the Garveses' ball. I, myself, was got up in layers and layers of pink net, "like the petals of a peony," Aunt Louise said, so that when I sat down I took three times the space a normal person would.

We had been invited to the Garves's for a small dinner for a hundred or so preceding the ball. I was seated next to Joey, and he grinned as he said, "I have such lovely memories of our afternoon together yesterday."

Overhearing his son, Brigadier General Garves said, "I suppose you children were at one of your tennis parties or out riding in the park?"

"Nothing so strenuous, Father," Joey told him. Across the table, Jane covered her face with her napkin to hide her laughter. I could not laugh. It was such a close call. If it hadn't been for the kindly judge who knew Raman's father, I would have been disgraced for life.

There were nearly as many footmen handing food about as guests consuming it. Halfway through the dinner a shiver of excitement went round the table. People whispered. Mr. Garves looked smug. Mrs. Garves appeared flushed and expectant. Even the servants looked about them as if something amazing was about to happen. As the last crumb of a *gâteau citron* was consumed and the women rose from the table to allow the men some peace and a glass of port, Jane drew me aside.

"I've been sworn to secrecy, but I know I can depend on you not to tell. You'll never guess who is coming to the ball." Before I could open my mouth and hazard a guess, Jane looked about and then whispered in my ear, "Their Majesties, King George and Queen Mary. They don't usually attend balls, but Father has just done the king a great service. Father arranged for a ship to sail to Greece to pick up the king's cousins, Prince and Princess Andrew, who were swept off the throne of Greece and might have been done in. The government didn't want us to get mixed up in the Greek revolution, but Father smoothed things over. Anyhow, as a sort of reward the king and queen are going to grace our ball with their presence, and everyone is too thrilled."

I was thrilled myself. It had been amazing to meet the Prince of Wales, but now here was a chance I would actually be at a party with the king of England. Of course there would be hundreds of people there and no chance to say a word to his majesty. Still, it would be something to brag about in my next letter to Max.

With the dinner over, the other guests began to arrive for the ball. There were two orchestras, a small one playing sedately to elderly people in a small room, and the other musicians making a great racket in the ballroom, where Joey, as soon as he spotted me, hurried across the room to pull me out onto the dance floor. He twirled me about, making me dizzy, and galloped me up and down until I was breathless.

Suddenly, the music stopped and everyone stood perfectly still as if some spell had fallen over us. All eyes were turned toward the entrance of the ballroom. There stood the king and queen, looking exactly like their pictures, the king with his neatly trimmed whiskers and the queen with fetching little curls all over her head. The orchestra struck up "God Save the King," and we stood at attention. The king and queen then processed along an informal reception line with all the women bobbing up and down and the men bowing and clicking their heels. After the little parade, the king waved a hand in the direction of the orchestra and, going up to Mrs. Garves, led her onto the dance floor. The others applauded and then joined the couple, Mr. Garves escorting Queen Mary.

Even Joey was impressed, and I felt a decided slowing of his tempo. "The old boy puts on quite a show," he said. "Father's been on a shooting with him. He said they got a thousand pheasants all in one day. Pretty impressive, I'd say."

"I think it sounds horrible, and if I have a chance, I'll tell him so."

"Oh, you'll never get within a mile of the old man. They'll all be so thick about him he won't have a chance to breathe."

Jane had told me that her parents had insured the success of the ball by inviting three young men for every girl, and I was never off the dance floor. I longed for a breath of air, and making my excuses to a young man who kept telling me how jolly everything was—jolly food, jolly music, jolly girls—I slipped out of the ballroom and made my way through the great doors that opened onto the veranda.

It was an entirely different world. Though the house was in Mayfair, in the heart of London, beyond the veranda was a small walled garden. Looking out at the dark silhouettes of the trees, listening to the splash of a fountain, I had such a longing for India. A rustling amongst the bushes interrupted the peaceful moment. *A wild dog,* I thought, *or burglars about to steal all the jewels on show.*

"Dear girl, you are not to give me away. The men think I am on the dance floor, and the queen thinks me at the billiard table with the men. The truth is, I had to get my shoe off. I have a touch of gout, don't you know, and the shoe fell into the bushes, and I can't seem to put a hand on it."

I dropped down into the curtsy of all curtsies. "Your Majesty."

"Never mind all that sort of thing. You're young and bendable and probably have good eyesight. I wonder if you would just have a look. I can't go back in there to that crowd without a shoe."

I picked up my skirts and dove into the bushes, careful to keep the net from getting caught in the branches. In moments I had the shoe.

"Well done, my dear. Now tell me your name and who you belong to."

"I'm Rosalind James, sir, and my father is a civil servant in India, where we live, and I am just here to be presented to you." I couldn't help laughing. "I don't suppose this counts."

"No, indeed. You must have feathers and all the proper rigmarole. I've a great fondness for India. I was there as a young man. They had a durbar for me, you know, a great celebration. It was 1911. I had to get all dressed up in ermine robes and white stockings in all that heat and sit on a golden throne. It was quite a sight, if I say so myself. They held umbrellas over me to keep out the worst of the sun, and they had young lads all dressed up in britches and turbans to work the fans. The queen had to wear long, white kid gloves. Ah, but what a parade they put on. The *maharajas* were more regal than I was with all their jewels and their fine golden carriages. You never saw such a show. Every so often I get out the paintings of the durbar that were made at the time and show my children so that they will be properly impressed by their father. I hope things are going along there pretty well."

"Oh no, sir. Everything's a muddle. The Indian people want their freedom from England." Too late it occurred to me that what I was saying was the Indian people wanted freedom from England and the king who ruled over them. What would the king have to say about that?

"Nonsense. I am sure we treat the Indian people very well. I was telling you just now how fond I am of the country. I'm their emperor as well as the king of England. People here are happy with that. Why shouldn't the people of India be content?"

"But, sir, it's quite different. Here in England you have the Houses of Parliament that make the laws for your country. In India it's England that makes the laws for the Indian people. That isn't fair."

"What did you say your name was? Rosalind, I believe.

Well, Rosalind, I have just been to France and Belgium, visiting the graves of the brave soldiers who died for England in the last war. It was the saddest trip of my life. I want no more unpleasantness between countries. India and England must get along."

"I don't know how they can get along when you put Gandhi, who is their leader, in jail and don't even let him have pencil and paper. I don't think that's fair."

"Yes, yes, I agree there. The man ought to be able to put down his thoughts, however misinformed they are. But tell me, why is a charming young woman worrying herself about such matters? You ought to be in there dancing with young men."

"Sir, if I were, you would not have your shoe."

"Ah, you have me there, and youth must have its dreams." The king put the shoe on and tied the lace. I noticed he did double bows and felt quite secure about the future of England, but less so about the freedom of India. "Now I must go into the ballroom and collect the queen. I intend to return to the palace, put up my foot, and have a nice cold glass of milk and a plain biscuit. I can't eat all this fancy food. Bad for the gout. In return for your good deed with the shoe I will drop a word about pen and paper for your friend Mr. Gandhi, and I will look

feathers."

With that, the king lifted himself off the bench and, brushing off his uniform and giving his whiskers a pat, disappeared through the doors into the ballroom. My time with the king had been more like a dream than the real thing, except I remembered the feel of the king's shoe in my hand and the gray that had crept into the king's well-groomed beard. I truly had been chatting away with England's sovereign, telling him how to rule his own country. The thing was, I liked him. I didn't want to make him unhappy, but I loved India. I don't know where I got the courage to say what I said to him, but I wasn't the least bit sorry, and I wished I'd had time for a word about the killing of all those pheasants.

A moment later, Joey burst through the doors and gathered me up as if I were a small dog who had wandered from the premises. "Whatever are you doing out here? Cooling off, I dare say. Excellent idea, but let's do it properly."

He led me across the veranda, onto the grass, and to the fountain, where he proceeded to roll up his trousers and take off his shoes and socks. In a moment he was wading about in the fountain. It took me only a second to shed my own shoes and stockings and hoist my skirts. The water was delightfully cool, and we stamped about and had a glorious time. Afterward, we sat on the ledge of the fountain and dried off. When it came time to put on our shoes and stockings, Joey complained, "Lost my shoe."

"Here it is," I said. Twice in the last hour I had hunted and found a lost shoe. I longed to tell Joey about the other shoe, but I didn't want to let go of my adventure. Joey and Jane would make a great joke out of it, and the magic would disappear. One day I would tell someone, Aunt Louise or Max or Raman, but for now the adventure was all mine.

21

Aunt Louise had her own adventure at the ball. Colonel Brighten had been there from Oxford. Next afternoon, he was at our door causing the usual mix of excitement and despair. Aunt Ethyl, whom I had never heard utter a word of criticism about England, now spoke discouragingly of the cold nights and dirty streets in London. "Everything is so much more comfortable in India," she said, something she did not believe for a moment, but I knew she would say anything to be sure that her sister returned with her to India and did not marry the colonel.

Mother was charming, pouring out tea and telling the colonel how much the children in the orphanage depended on Aunt Louise. "I don't know how they would ever get along without you, Louise. I know you have had many letters from Mrs. Nelson telling you how much you are missed." Mother had no intention of allowing her much-loved sister to remain behind in England.

On the other hand, Father thought all women ought to be married or how could they possibly manage. As he munched the seed cake Rita had prepared for our tea, Father spoke of the charm of living in a university town. "I envy you, colonel, residing in Oxford, all those libraries and museums and bright young men scooting about. Very stimulating to the mind."

"You are so correct, James. I wonder if we couldn't manage a little visit for Louise. I would like to show her the charms of Oxford myself."

In no time Father arranged for Joey to escort us to Oxford so Aunt Louise could visit Colonel Brighten. The next Saturday, Joey came down from Oxford, gathered Aunt Louise and me, and took us by train up to Balliol College, where he was a student and the colonel the headmaster.

Oxford was called the city of dreaming spires, and it was quite true. Everywhere we looked, the spires of the colleges and churches rose up over the city. The headmaster's home was set on a field of green grasses and looked perfectly settled, as if it had been there for a hundred years, as indeed it had.

The colonel greeted our little party of three on his doorstep, graciously inviting us in. After warm greetings for Aunt Louise and myself, he gazed upon Joey with increasing recognition. "Ah, yes. Young Garves. Your tutor reports you have a sharp mind and a dull sense of responsibility. I believe you are also in a spot of trouble for interrupting a speaker by letting loose a cage of chickens in the university auditorium."

"I'm most terribly sorry about that, sir. The speaker had talked drivel about hanging on to all of England's colonies. I wanted to get across the fact that I thought his ideas foul—you know, *fowl*."

"Yes, yes, Garves, I am not so dense that I need an explanation for your pranks. Next time try words instead of chickens. Now, I understand I am to put this young woman in your care while I visit with Mrs. Hartley. I frankly tremble at the thought of her in your hands, and I warn you, Garves, that should there be any little difficulty, today will be your last in this college."

Joey took me off at once to the river. "You don't want

to spend the afternoon with a lot of smelly, stupid students. I've engaged a boat and laid on a picnic for us."

We climbed into a small rowboat, Joey produced a basket, and we pushed off from the dock. He was an enthusiastic oarsman, and in no time we had followed the Thames River past Christ Church Meadow. We were going along very nicely when I exclaimed over some apple blossoms.

"You shall have them," Joey said, and guiding the boat under the branches that stretched out over the water, he reached up a little too far into the branches of the apple tree, and the boat tipped over with us in it.

We stood soaked to the skin and knee deep in the river, the branch of blossoms still in Joey's hand. He said, "Can't take you back like a drowned rat and present you to the headmaster, leaking water on his doorstep. You'll have to come to my rooms and dry off."

We righted the boat, and dripping all the way, sneaked back through the colleges to Balliol and, when no one was looking, dashed up the ancient stairway to Joey's rooms. "Tell you what, old girl, I'll start a fire in my fireplace, and then I'll sneak off to the rooms of a friend. You peel off and dry your clothes."

Left alone in Joey's rooms with a fire going, I turned

a huge old key to lock the door and climbed out of my clothes, which I wrung and arranged in front of the fire. I was wrapped in a shirt of Joey's, examining the books in his bookcase, some of which were written by revolutionaries such as Marx and Engels, but there were quite a few racy novels and a copy of *The Wind in the Willows*. There was a knock at the door. I heard Colonel Brighten's voice, "Garves, its Brighten here and Miss Hartley."

I held my breath. There I was in Joey's room with my clothes off. Of course he wasn't there, but how convincing would my explanation be? They would think he had climbed out the window. Even if they believed me, how would they feel about our having been in the river? I didn't dare let them into the room. After a bit, I heard them heading down the stairway, and I breathed again.

When Joey and I went to collect Aunt Louise, the colonel scrutinized us. "Well, you two seem all in one piece. We did try to pay you a visit, thinking you might be having tea in your rooms, but there was no answer. I trust you had a pleasant afternoon's stroll though the school and perhaps took in the museum."

"We did a bit of exploring of the countryside, sir. I just hope it wasn't boring for Miss James."

"Not at all, Joey," I said with perfect composure.

We had a compartment to ourselves in the train, and I asked Aunt Louise if she had had a pleasant visit with Colonel Brighten.

"I did enjoy it, Rosy. He is the nicest man. He took me about and showed me all the colleges. His own college is over six hundred years old. Imagine that. The colonel was greeted everywhere by the students in such a friendly way. I met some of the fellows from his college and one or two of their wives as well. The colonel explained to me everyone's position. It's all quite formal, you see. One dines with those who hold a similar position." Aunt Louise paused and looked out of the train window at the backyards of a row of houses. "Another thing, Rosy. Right there in front of the colonel's college the Archbishop of Canterbury, Thomas Cranmer, the man who wrote the English book of prayer that I am so fond of—right there on Broad Street, Cranmer was burned to death for his religious beliefs. Of course that was three hundred fifty years ago, but even so. I wonder if I could speak freely there, for many of the tutors were once in India as members of the British government."

After another silence, Aunt Louise said, "You know, Rosy, I am counting the days to our return to India. Everything is so simple there. I have my work at the orphanage, and there is the excitement of the bazaar and all the dreams of freedom for India. I could never settle down to a town like Oxford and the routine of a headmaster's wife."

And whatever doubts or thoughts Aunt Louise had, the colonel was never mentioned again.

Jane and I and our mothers spent hours shopping for the clothes we would wear at the presentation. You didn't wear just what you liked, but what was the custom. You were required to have a long train dragging from your dress and a veil of tulle like a bride, the tulle stretched out behind you, covering the train. Then there were the dreaded ostrich feathers, which had been sent to me. There needed to be three of them, and they were arranged in strict order, with the tallest in the middle and two shorter ones on either side. The problem with the feathers was they were hard to attach and with a rigorous curtsy often came unattached and floated away.

Jane and I were determined not to lose our feathers and drove hairpins into our scalps in a ferocious way to keep them in place. The other thing was the curtsy. It wasn't just a quick dip but a full court curtsy that meant you went down on one knee nearly to the floor and then, while you were trying to keep from toppling over, you had to incline your head, along with the feathers, in a graceful nod at the sovereigns. After all that, you rose up again and, never turning your back on the king and queen, made your way backward somehow managing the long train.

We practiced every day, and our screams of laughter were so loud, Mrs. Garves had to warn us of the seriousness of the event. "It will be the highlight of your young lives, girls, and you must take it seriously. After all, it is the king and queen!"

We tried to suppress our laughter, but Jane would trip over her train or I would see my feathers floating away, and we would end up in gales of laughter and Mrs. James would be once more at the door admonishing us. I suppose it was very frivolous and I'm sure Max would not have approved, but I had never had a close girlfriend like Jane, and her laughter got me through what could have been a very dull time.

We practiced our backward walking everywhere and became quite good at walking down the stairway backward and were often seen on the pathways of Hyde Park walking backward, much to the astonishment of the onlookers.

It was all great fun, which we never took seriously until the day of the presentation, when we sat with our mothers in the Garveses' Rolls-Royce, part of a long line of other cars. The line moved slowly, and it seemed our turn would never come. With each moment I was more and more unsure of my deportment. I was convinced I would trip over my train. I would certainly topple while trying to kneel. And experienced as I was at backward walking, how would I switch my train around when it was time to make an exit? Our mothers tried to comfort us, but they were as nervous as we were.

At last it was our turn. Young men serving as ushers led us into the palace and to the gallery where we were to be presented. Jane went in first, leaving me to imagine all the awful things that could happen. Then it was my turn. I hardly knew what I was doing, but a pleasant young usher took a firm grip on my arm and all but lifted me into the presentation room. When I paused at the entrance, terrified, the usher gave me a gentle push forward.

There, sitting on a sort of dais, were the king and queen looking absolutely serious, if not a bit irritated, although they might simply have been tired or bored. Helped by the usher's little shove, I walked as gracefully as I could

237

toward the sovereigns. I made my curtsy, dipping almost to the floor, at which point my knee cracked and I was sure the sound echoed all over the room. But, no, there was no laughter. I inclined my head, paused, and then began to rise, only to see one of my feathers rising on its own mission. I was horrified, but a very nice attendant dashed over and swooped it up.

At that moment, my face burning, I looked up at the king. There was a faint smile on his face, and I saw him wiggle his shoe. Another usher dashed out to help switch the train, and I backed quite gracefully out of the room and collapsed in my mother's arms, half laughing and half crying.

The usher returned my lost feather with a deep bow and a grin, and I and Jane, who had gotten through it perfectly, were carried off with our mothers, who were as relieved as we were. During the presentation, I had forgotten the king's role in India and had just thought of him as the nice man on the veranda, and when he had wiggled his shoe, I could have hugged him.

After the presentation, even Aunt Ethyl was ready to return to India. I heard her whisper to Aunt Louise, "I haven't had my corset off for a month." Our trunks were overflowing with all of our purchases. I wanted to leave my presentation gown and train behind, but Aunt Ethyl said, "Nonsense. It will do quite nicely for your wedding, and you won't find anything so fine in India." So in went the train and the veil but not the feathers. Jane and I took our feathers to Hyde Park and sent them out over the Serpentine. They wafted along for a few moments and then settled like six white swans on the water and drifted away. Jane and I pledged our friendship forever, and Jane promised to visit me soon in India. "I'll bring Joey, shall I? And we'll get up a proper revolution."

Of course I would love to see Jane and Joey, too, in India, but I wondered what Max would make of them. There are colorful flowers you pluck to enjoy, but somehow, once taken from the garden, they lose their brightness.

All that was left was to say good-bye to Raman. It was a sunny May day, and I arrived at the Inner Temple by one of London's cabs. In India I would miss the comfortable cabs with their friendly drivers. How much kinder to be pulled about by an engine than by a miserable man with the weight of your *tonga* on his shoulders. I met Raman

in the gardens of the Inner Temple. Roses bloomed everywhere, and the lawn was greener than any lawn in India,
where the cruel sun scorched everything. Raman pointed
out an ancient rookery. "It's been there for years and years.
The crows in their black feathers look remarkably like the
barristers in their black robes."

Seated in the secluded gardens, we were in the middle
of the busy city, the great dome of St. Paul's cathedral visible
behind us and the Victoria Embankment and the Thames
River nearby. We sat next to each other, Raman so close I
could feel the warmth of his body. "I've decided my father
was right to send me here," he said.

"But you once told me your writing for *Young India*
was more important."

"I've changed my mind. I've learned to care for this
place and what it stands for. Do you know just last week
a very pleasant woman named Ivy Williams became England's first woman barrister? She was called to the bar right
here at the Inner Temple."

I was a little jealous of this "very pleasant woman"
whom Raman admired, but it turned out she was forty-
four, practically ancient.

"It's more than that," Raman said. "I haven't forgotten

that Gandhi trained to be a barrister here at the Temple when he was younger than I am. England is a country of laws, and I'll learn to make use of those laws to give India its freedom."

"How long must you stay here?"

"All the rest of this year, and then additional time to get some actual practice, but Father has said I can come home for a visit, and your friends Joey and Jane have pledged to keep me occupied." He turned to me with a smile. "I suppose I'll return to find Max has scooped you up while I'm away. At least promise me you won't be involved in one of Max's wild schemes."

"If I am, you can be my barrister and get me out of jail. Anyhow, you are more likely to get into trouble with Jane and Joey than I am with Max." To tell the truth, I wasn't at all happy to leave Raman in Jane's hands.

We walked together to the Embankment and looked over at the Thames. The river was busy with pleasure boats and barges and a great ship that was perhaps headed for India. The next day I would board our own ship. Now it was not just what I would be sailing toward but what I would be leaving behind. I thought about Ivy Williams and told myself that I might return to England and to the

Inner Temple and, like Raman, become a barrister. I saw myself in a black gown and a white wig, and I saw Raman and myself back in India together, pleading for Gandhi's innocence, getting him out of prison and then working for India's freedom. Of course that would be years away, and in the meantime I had a letter in my pocket from Max.

Dear Rosy,

All is well here. Hari is thriving with his parents. Sajala has grown brave and is practically running the orphanage. I drop by your house every once in a while when I am especially lonesome for you, and I can report that the trees and flowers and monkeys are all languishing while they await your return. I've tried to hold a few classes for your young students, but I find the students distracting me with questions and lizards so that lessons never get done.

While you have been consorting with kings
and queens our struggle for India's freedom
has been going on. Of course you have no
way of knowing, but you will be pleased
to learn that for some mysterious reason
Gandhi has at last been allowed pencil and
paper. Because of that happy event, he is
writing all kinds of powerful articles that
we print in _Young India._

I miss you, and I need you for an amazing
scheme that is only a little dangerous and
for which I must have your help.

Hurry home,

Max

I couldn't wait.

Author's Note

After finishing *Small Acts of Amazing Courage*, I continued to wonder about Rosalind and what trouble her convictions and good intentions might cause her, how her Aunt Ethyl would get along in India, what Aunt Louise was doing, and what was happening to Gandhi's dream of freedom for India.

When I learned that in 1921, two years after *Small Acts of Amazing Courage* ended, the Prince of Wales would be in India, I began to imagine what that might mean to Rosalind. Lord Louis Mountbatten, who accompanied the prince, kept a journal of his trip to India. He set down day by day all the glamour and excitement of India: the unbelievably wealthy *maharajas*, the daily receptions and parties, the tiger hunts. And I saw that the prince would be in Calcutta, very near Rosalind. I longed to bring them together.

At the time of the prince's visit, Gandhi called for a *hartal*, a strike, to close down Indian participation in British institutions. When the Prince of Wales landed on the shore of India, he was met with both the cheers of British loyalists and the anger of those Indians who resented the British hold on their country. How could I not put Rosalind in the middle of so exciting a time? And, then, why could she not meet the king himself? The letter Rosalind presents to the Prince of Wales is authentic. It was published on October 20, 1920, in *Young India*, a magazine started by Gandhi. My source for the letter is the Bombay Sarvodaya Mandal and the Gandhi Research Foundation www.mkgandhi.org/ias.htm.

While we know the Prince of Wales, Lord Louis, and King George III were very real people, we also know that Rosalind and the other characters, as well as the places, were imagined. But we can hope that somewhere in India at that time a young girl like Rosy dreamed about meeting the prince and telling him India's story. And we can hope she did!

Dickie, Lord Louis Mountbatten, a young man of twenty-one, seeing India for the first time in 1921, surely didn't imagine that a quarter of a century later, on August 15, 1947, as the viceroy of India, he would be the man who at long last gave India its freedom.

Five months later, on January 30, 1948, Mohandas Gandhi, who was more responsible than any other man for India's freedom, was assassinated by a Hindu extremist while on his way to a prayer meeting.

Ganghi's letter from *Young India* magazine, published October 20, 1920, in its entirety.

To Every Englishman in India

Dear Friend,

I wish that every Englishman will see this appeal and give thoughtful attention to it.

Let me introduce myself to you. In my humble opinion no Indian has co-operated with the British Government more than I have for an unbroken period of twenty-nine years of public life in the face of circumstances that might well have turned any other man into a rebel. I ask you to believe me when I tell you that my co-operation was not based on the fear of the punishments provided by your laws or any other selfish motives. It is free and voluntary co-operation based on the belief that the sum total of the British Government was for the benefit of India. I put my life in peril four times for the sake of the Empire,—at the time of the Boer War when I was in charge of the Ambulance corps whose work was mentioned in the General Buller's dispatches, at the time of the Zulu revolt in Natal when I was in charge of a similar corps, at the time of the commencement of the late War when I raised an Ambulance Corps and as a result of the strenuous training had a severe attack of pleurisy and, lastly, in fulfillment of my promise to Lord Chelmsford at the War Conference in Delhi, I threw myself in such an active recruiting campaign in Kaira District involving long and trying marches that I had an attack of dysentery which proved almost fatal. I did all this in the full belief that acts such as mine must gain

my country an equal status in the Empire.
So last December I pleaded hard for the
trustful co-operation. I fully believed
that Mr. Lloyd George would redeem his
promise to the Mussulmans and that the
revelations of the official atrocities in the
Punjab would secure full reparation for the
Punjabis. But the treachery of Mr. Lloyd
George and its appreciation by you, and
the condonation of the Punjab atrocities,
have completely shattered my faith in the
good intentions of the Government and the
nation which is supporting it.

But though my faith in your good
intentions is gone, I recognise your
bravery and I know that what you will not
yield to justice and reason, you will gladly
yield to bravery.

See what this Empire means to India:

Exploitations of India's resources for the benefit of Great Britain.

An ever-increasing military expenditure, and a civil service the most expensive in the world.

Extravagant working of every department in utter disregard of India's poverty.

Disarmament and consequent emasculation of a whole nation, lest an armed nation might imperil the lives of a handful of you in our midst.

Traffic in intoxicating liquors and drugs for the purpose of sustaining a top-heavy administration.

Progressively repressive legislation in order to Suppress an ever-growing agitation, seeking to give expression to a nation's agony.

Degrading treatment of Indians residing in your dominions, and,

You have shown total disregard of our feelings by glorifying the Punjab administration and flouting the Mussulman sentiment.

I know you would not mind if we could fight and wrest the scepter from your hands. You know that we are powerless to do that, for you have ensured our incapacity to fight in open and honourable battle. Bravery on the battlefield is thus impossible for us. Bravery of the soul still remains open to us. I know you will respond to that also. I am engaged in evoking that bravery. Non-co-operation means nothing less than training in self-sacrifice. Why

should we co-operate with you when we
know that, by your administration of
this great country, we are being daily
enslaved in an increasing degree? This
response of the people to my appeal is not
due to my personality. I would like you to
dismiss me, and for that matter the Ali
Brothers too, from your consideration. My
personality will fail to evoke any response
to anti-Muslim cry if I were foolish
enough to raise it, as the magic name of
the Ali Brothers would fail to inspire the
Mussulmans with enthusiasm if they were
madly to raise an anti-Hindu cry. People
flock in their thousands to listen to us
because we today represent the voice of a
nation groaning under your iron heels. The
Ali Brothers were your friends as I was,
and still am. My religion forbids me to
bear any ill-will towards you. I would not
raise my hand against you even if I had the

power. I expect to conquer you only by my suffering. The Ali Brothers will certainly draw the sword if they could, in defense of their religion and their country. But they and I have made common cause with the people of India in their attempt to voice their feelings and to find a remedy for their distress.

You are in search of a remedy to suppress this rising ebullition of national feeling. I venture to suggest to you that the only way to suppress it is to remove the causes. You have yet the power. You can repent of the wrongs done to Indians. You can compel Mr. Lloyd George to redeem his promises. I assure you he has kept many escape doors. You can compel the Viceroy to retire in favour of a better one, you can revise your ideas about Sir Michael O'Dwyer and General Dyer. You can compel the government to summon a conference of the recognised leaders of the people duly elected by them and representing all shades of opinion so as to devise means for granting <u>Swaraj</u> in accordance with the wishes of the people of India.

But this you cannot do unless you consider every Indian to be in reality your equal and brother. I ask for no patronage. I merely point out to you, as a friend, an honourable solution of a grave problem. The other solution, namely, repression is open to you. I prophesy that it will fail. It has begun already. The Government has already imprisoned two brave men of Panipat for holding and expressing their opinions freely. Another is on his trial in Lahore for having expressed similar opinions. One in the Oudh District is already imprisoned. Another awaits judgment. You should know what is going on in your midst. Our propaganda is being carried on in anticipation of repression. I invite you respectfully to choose the better way and make common cause with the people of India whose salt you are eating. To seek to thwart their aspirations is disloyalty to the country.

I am,.

Your faithful friend,.

M. K. Gandhi

Originally published November 27, 1920, in *Young India*

Glossary

annas: *coinage that makes up a shilling*

ayah: *nursemaid*

burra mali: *head servant*

chapati: *a flat bread*

charkha: *spinning wheel*

charpoy: *wooden bed frame laced with rope*

chota mali: *assistant servant*

chula: *a grill*

congee: *rice porridge*

Glossary

ghee: *clarified butter*

godown: *warehouse*

hartal: *a nonviolent strike called by Gandhi*

halwa: *a dessert*

jinn: *an evil spirit*

kameez: *a shirt or blouse*

karma: *fate, destiny*

khadi: *a homespun cloth*

khichdi: *rice with lentils*

kurta: *a long shirt*

lassi: *an iced drink made with yogurt and fruits and spices*

Glossary

maidan: *parade ground and field for sports*

Memsahib: *Mrs. or Mistress*

namaste: *greeting made by holding the palms together*

nimbu pani: *fresh lime juice*

pagari: *a kind of turban*

poppadum: *flat crispy bread*

pukka: *correct, behaving in a traditional way*

salwar: *loose-fitting trousers*

sass: *mother-in-law*

sassur: *father-in-law*

shikanji: *a spicy lemon drink*

Glossary

tonga: *a cab pulled by a person or horse to transport people through the streets*

zenana: *the part of the house designated just for women*

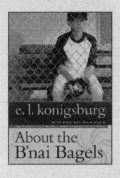